I know : stories

T H I

P E O P

I

K N O W

WINNER

OF

THE

FLANNERY

O'CONNOR

AWARD

FOR

SHORT

FICTION

THE

PEOPLE

I

KNOW

STORIES
BY NANCY
ZAFRIS

THE

UNIVERSITY

OF GEORGIA

PRESS

ATHENS AND

LONDON

Published in 2009 by the University of Georgia Press
Athens, Georgia 30602
www.ugapress.org
© 1990 by Nancy Zafris
All rights reserved
Designed by Richard Hendel
Set in Pilgrim

Printed digitally in the United States of America

The Library of Congress has cataloged the hardcover
edition of this book as follows:

Zafris, Nancy.
    The people I know : stories / by Nancy Zafris.
    v, 162 p. ; 23 cm.
    "Winner of the Flannery O'Connor Award for Short Fiction."
    ISBN 0-8203-1192-8 (alk. paper)
    1. United States—Social life and customs—20th century—
Fiction. I. Title.
PS3576.A285P6 1990
813'.54—dc20   89-34553

Paperback ISBN-13: 978-0-8203-3420-2
        ISBN-10: 0-8203-3420-0

British Library Cataloging-in-Publication Data available

"The People I Know" previously appeared in the *Black Warrior Review* and in *Into the Silence*, an anthology published by Green Street Press. "Cosmetic Surgery" and "A Minor Fatality" were first published in the *Black Warrior Review*. "Final Weeks" first appeared in *Hawaii Review*.

CONTENTS

THE

PEOPLE

I

KNOW

C O S M E T I C

S U R G E R Y

What a name she was given, Pavla Sobolewski. But she was smart enough to change it to Wendy. The original name suited her Old World looks; she was handsome rather than pretty. The nose was strong and full of history, but it was not what young girls wanted. She thought everyone looked at her a little taken aback, as if thinking to themselves, You look like a Pavla, not a Wendy.

In her early twenties she became more of what a Wendy should look like: streaked brown hair, a contemporary nose, thinner eyebrows. If not Californian, she at least looked American and not salvaged from the Baltic Sea. People, she imagined, were no longer taken aback. She could relax. That she had always received peculiar pleasure from bestowing a name prettier than what her face deserved was something she didn't realize until the pleasure was gone. She could no longer think about her face without getting bored.

Once her face was pretty, she tried turning it back into ugly with punk hairdos and cosmetics. But it wasn't the same. She couldn't recapture the feeling. Recapturing the feeling was a problem she was having with a lot of things.

Even so young, she was full of untimely obituaries. She watched each year contribute to a growing casualty list. Death of her face. Death of pleasure from being slightly ugly. Death of social embarrassment. Death of gustatory excitement. Great passions of a year ago lacked so much as the tingle of taste you get from licking a postage stamp.

Her love of literature, for example. There was a time when she would give up sleep for it. She could bear so little the

thought of parting with *David Copperfield* that when she finished she simply returned to the first page and started again.
She had a hard time impressing upon people the exact way
she had flipped the book over, as if turning a page, so that the
final page melted into the first. She found it hard explaining
to them that the sentence "Whether I shall turn out to be the
hero of my own life . . . ," famous though it was, was not
actually the first sentence. It was the second sentence.

She believed sincerely that this method of treating *Copperfield* was proof enough she was graduate school material,
although once she made it, her success, like her new face,
turned against her. Now when her classmates spoke of an
author's point of departure, she thought of an airport and the
verb "to deplane." When a professor mentioned deconstruc-
tionism, she thought of cranes and demolition balls. And if
someone said "madeleine," she thought of food. Lots of it.
Death of gustatory excitement came the following year. This
year witnessed the death of love of literature.

When she fell in love, she thought her problem was solved.
New, intense feelings were awakened. The man, whom she
later married, reminded her of a falcon: his face was swift
and lean, his hair combed straight back from a widow's peak.
The springiness of his build promised an athleticism he did
not possess. There were other promises he did not make and
which he thus failed to fulfill. Eventually, and for no reason,
she found herself disappointed.

At a trade show she attended (death of literature had led
to the business world), she rode from the airport to the hotel
with a man from the marketing group of her company. She
was fascinated—against her will, as it were—by the ease
with which he liked himself. Men who liked themselves, she
noticed, tended to keep their hands in their pockets, jangling
their change as if their pennies were bonus testicles. She felt
a brief thrill as she talked with him in the hotel lobby and

listened to the sound of his coins. When his hands weren't in his pockets, they were smoothing the length of his tie or touching her elbow to punctuate a remark.

She liked the fact that even attentive listening in these marketing guys was a skill they splashed on like cologne. His particular brand stayed on her the rest of the day. It was even on the drinks she brought to her lips at the reception that night. When he waved to her, it was as if he had been with her all these hours, except now he was closer. He had poured on a refresher of cologne. His scent was almost overpowering when he stood so near. It was strange the sway it had over her. It made her think seriously about things she normally wouldn't consider. It made her think that infidelity was no big thing. I am not being unfaithful, she told herself. No more than if I used a deodorized tampon.

She walked away to consider the matter further. She considered where she was in life. These yearly deaths of feeling had scarred her soul. Annual tree rings grew around her spirit. You could count the rings and guess her age by what she was not. There were twenty rings devoted just to her nose. But she could hardly believe that she had ever worried about her face, that she used to dream of good test scores, that she had fallen in love, that anything had ever made her heart speed past its textbook 72 a minute. Things were dead and buried. If the current aging process continued, with each year seeing another passion thrown like a corpse toward a ditch, she would grow up into a zombie by age thirty-five. She owed it to herself not to retreat from anything that might bring her back to life.

Because she had never had an affair, it was the details leading up to the actual step inside the bedroom that were the most excruciating, and therefore the most pleasant: violation of her airspace during conversation, increased elbow touching whenever he said, "And get this, Wendy . . . ," being escorted to the elevator and then to her bedroom. She could tell it was not a new experience with him, and yet he was still excited by it. She was excited by it too, but for precisely the opposite reason.

The sensation of being intimate with someone she normally wouldn't like was a unique one. His marketing mannerisms in the taxi had been fun to watch. Naked and in bed, he was even more fun to watch. Theater of the real is what she thought. The guy loved to perform. But limited to one, as his audience was, he could increase the membership only by multiplying the performances. So she was good for just one night. That was fine with her. The things he said and did in bed were hilarious. That, and her own overwhelming fear, were exhilarating. It was a unique distillation, like his cologne. But as soon as it was over, she knew it couldn't be duplicated. Breakfast was boring: he was already looking for the next member of his audience, and she was already growing moss around the experience.

By the time she arrived home, even the memory of her fear had evaporated. She panicked. So much deadwood. Tree rings squeezed around her like a corset. She thought she might suffocate.

Then she had a stay of execution: she felt guilt. The guilt for what she had done was surprisingly affecting, enough that she felt compelled to do it again and relive the experience simultaneous with the piercing of guilt, which she didn't have the first time. It worked. The guilt and the forbidden infidelity and the sexual act itself combined to create a feeling so intense that her partner must have sensed it, for he suddenly turned her on her stomach where she could be alone with it and entered her from behind. It was exactly what she wanted. For a minute she thought they were kindred spirits; then she realized there were other reasons for what she thought was a charitable act. Unless she was willing for complete darkness and a pillow always in her face, the affair couldn't continue.

The guilt had left anyway. Now, during various couplings so brief they couldn't properly be termed affairs, her mind wandered. She thought of things like the word "hermeneutics" and the phrase "pleasures of the text." There was a longer affair with a man named Matthew, which caused anxiety at first because she had never had to lie to her husband more than once. For a while it was very pleasant, until she realized she was anxious over nothing. Half the time she forgot she was even married; anxiety was something she had willed.

Matthew wore the same outfit every day. He had a closet full of khaki pants and blue workshirts. That was all he wore, but each outfit, although the same, was different. It was his way of getting attention, she supposed, and it worked, at least with her. She was attracted to it. It reminded her of her own clothing habits. In her closet she always hung a new blouse that she didn't wear. She couldn't wear it because she knew it would look good on her. When, after a few weeks, she finally broke down and wore it, it looked better than good —it looked great. On the second day it looked good. After that it didn't look so good. She finally had to admit her disappointment and buy another new blouse that she never wore (until she broke down a few weeks or months later and the cycle repeated itself).

She ended the relationship with Matthew and decided she would remain celibate the rest of her life. Then the experience couldn't be over and thereby disappointing until she was old, and by then it wouldn't matter since she'd be about to die anyway.

It didn't work. Celibacy, an act of doing nothing, took more work than doing something. She took up with a man who had some of the same qualities as the marketing guy in the hope of recapturing some of the emotion from that first illicit affair. The trouble was that "first" and "illicit" were no longer operative adjectives. It was getting harder and harder to use those two words in front of any noun that applied to her. Of course, if pressed, she could find a way, but then it would just be ridiculous. The real trouble lay in replacing the word "ridiculous" with the word "exciting." Even thinking about it was tedious.

In John, the man she was currently seeing, she was attracted to that same phony quality as in the marketeer. But there was a major difference between them: John didn't say things like "And here's the kicker." He thought of himself as a connoisseur of the arts.

John, the connoisseur, loved gestures. Gestures that were subtle, sophisticated, and yet distinctly masculine. The ping of a briefcase lock. Opening it with both hands at the corners, the way hit men open their attaché cases, as if to emphasize precision rather than murder. Dressed in a suit, he loved the act of sitting down. As he bent over, he would unbutton his jacket in a single snap and make a smooth pass over his tie. He loved it most at restaurants when members of the group staggered in, forcing him to stand for the arriving guest, smooth his tie, button his jacket, smooth his tie, unbutton his jacket, sit down, and then stand back up and repeat it when the next person arrived.

It was at a restaurant that she had first met him. He was almost excessively polite to everyone except the one person to whom he was mean. That was his wife, and he was mean to her simply by not being excessively polite. He picked at his food while she talked instead of looking her deep in the eyes and nodding, as he did with everyone else. With the odd tone he had set, the aura of gesture, this simple lapse was somehow more offensive than if he had been overtly rude.

He was such a phony, but he wanted to be real (unlike the marketeer, who was a phony and also wanted to be one), and that was what stirred her blood and made her heartbeat go up to 75 or more. He asked her to lunch as he was helping her with her coat. His wife was perhaps two feet away and he seemed to make a point of asking her softly but loudly enough to be overheard. This added a new twist: being unfaithful to someone out loud while pretending to whisper a secret. Perhaps she had met someone who had the same problem? It was something to look forward to. Her heartbeat went up to 78.

She had two days to savor it before she sat outside the city's university and waited for him. Joggers stopped near her and splashed their faces with water from the fountain. At first she had been impressed with joggers. Three or four miles sounded like a lot. They sweated and it seemed exhilarating. Then she upped it to marathoners. Then only to marathoners who clocked in under two and a half hours. Lately even these fast marathoners had become slackers, people who could only do one-third of a triathlon. Triathletes got her emotions worked up for a while, until she saw an amputee do a triathlon, and then a man with diabetes. But the amputee didn't finish and the man with diabetes came in toward last. No reason for the diabetic not to sprint the whole way. Just up the insulin and do the whole thing in a sugar rush. The handicappers would have to do better. Triathlons were getting boring.

From where she sat, by the university fountain, she could watch the students bringing their food out of the cafeteria to eat on picnic tables or the stone steps. Most everyone appeared to be half-naked and beautiful. She realized for the first time that there was such a thing as a seventeen-year-old body and that she no longer had it. The girls with these bodies had faces to match. It surprised her that despite the twenty-year struggle with her own face she didn't find the effortlessness of their beauty annoying. That she didn't in some secret place envy them. It was true that she hardly gave them a thought, although no one would have believed her.

The people she found herself envying were those students who watched from the outside. Whatever it was that was wrong with them—fatness, ugliness, clumsiness, literalness

—it had allied itself early on with inexperience. Rather than do everything alone, they had just decided to sit it out for ten or fifteen years. They sat and watched the others. They ate their food as if glad for the company. Drugs, sex, that kind of stuff, was not even a question with them. They were on a level where maybe a kind word was like a shot of heroin. A kind act could get them through a whole decade.

She envied them. They could get excited about the stupidest things. And there were a lot of stupid things in the world. They had enough stupid things to keep them excited till about age seventy. She'd like to get that excited. But she couldn't. She was too smart.

THE
PEOPLE
I
KNOW

My mother is propped up in bed with the pillow shoved under her chest. She looks to be peering over the edge of a pool. This is how she always lies before she sleeps. Now she'll smoke cigarettes for at least an hour and talk to me until I drift off. Sometimes in fatigue she'll drop her head and smoke with one side of her face pressed against the mattress. With each puff she lifts her head slightly, like a swimmer catching air during his stroke, and blows the smoke away.

"Do you know what déjà vu is?" she asks me.

"Yes."

"I feel like I've got it all the time."

"You ought to. You do this every night," I say.

"Do what, baby?"

"Smoke, stare into space, tell me you've got déjà vu."

Without lifting her body, she wrestles the pillow from under her chest and smacks it on top of me. "I never told you I had it before."

I throw the pillow back to her.

"Maybe it's just déjà vu," she says, "for you." She bounces her hand in a piano-playing flourish to this rhyme and breaks into laughter. She's a heavy smoker and her laughter erupts in bursts of phlegm. She turns toward me and the hollows in her cheeks seem daubed with black paint. I feel hypnotized by those two holes of black; I realize, as if it's my last thought ever, that I'm a second away from sleep.

She leans over the aisle separating our beds and offers me her cigarette. I have barely enough strength to shake my head.

"What'd you say?" she asks.

"Nothing."

"What?"

I moan. "School," I try to whisper.

"What, baby?"

I can see I'm not getting out of this one easily. I gather my strength for one last sentence. "I never smoke after brushing my teeth." Then I'm gone.

If she could, she'd keep me up till dawn. She would like to sleep too, I think, but her body obeys the cranky rhythms of her mind. I am young, however, and my body still obeys its bodily needs. And so, right in the middle of her talk, I fall like a stone into shallow sleep. When I open my eyes, I don't know whether a few minutes or a few hours have passed: my mother has remained the same, staring, aiming her smoke over the top of the headboard. The coiling smoke has solidified into a thick gray cloud.

"You know what I'm thinking?" she says.

"Where are we now?"

"Him. We're back to him again." She means my father. "You know what I've been laying here thinking? That if I'd been smart like you I wouldn't have got duped."

"You're smart," I say. "Everyone says so."

"In medicine, baby. Along medical lines. That's not what I'm thinking about."

"Mmm."

"What?"

My eyes close.

"Okay, so don't answer me."

I jerk awake. "What was that?" The front door slams a second time.

"Sue's home. Lord help us."

"Mmm."

"Wait and see."

We hear a pot being thrown from the stove to the sink, then from the sink to the floor. Sue pounds up the stairs. "Here it starts," my mother whispers. Then Sue pounds down the stairs. The walls begin to shake with the sound of her stereo.

Sue is our roommate. It's hard to like Sue except in degrees. On the other hand, it's easy to dislike her wholeheartedly. She and my mother split the rent and try to share the apartment. It's not easy being in the middle of two thirty-six-year-old roommates. I watch them develop a hairline wrinkle one week, a gray hair the next, and in between regress just as fast as they're aging. Sue used to be a travel agent; now she's a waitress. My mother's a medical receptionist who has become increasingly sidetracked by schemes to get Sue's goat— calling from work to wake her up, signing her up for special offers she clips from *Parade*. This is a living arrangement I hope will end soon.

As music rattles the walls, Sue thumps up and down the steps. Against the noise of her stereo, this stomping emerges as trumpets in an orchestra, more felt than heard. Finally we hear a banging on our bedroom door. Sue sticks her head in. It's a small head; the shape of it in profile is all nose, no chin or forehead.

"Come in, Sue," my mother says.

"I can't stay," Sue says. "I just dropped in to remind you how many times I've asked you not to smoke while I'm home."

My mother takes a long drag before she answers. "When I can't sleep because someone's playing their stereo at 2 A.M., then I smoke."

"For God's sake! I work hard and I need to unwind!"

"The choice is yours."

"My God! You're so selfish!"

"Might I mention also," my mother continues in the excessively calm voice she affects with Sue, like a therapist with a neurotic patient, "that I have a daughter who attends high school early in the morning. Speaking of selfish, that is."

"Well, who could sleep with all this smoke? You can't even breathe."

"It's easier to sleep to the sound of smoke than to the sound of that music." By the way my mother takes a long indulgent suck on her cigarette, I can tell she thinks that was a damn good line. Sue slams the door and my mother rolls the cigarette around the rim of the ashtray. Sometimes she circles the whole rim. It's a habit of hers during contemplation. "What'd you think?" she asks.

"You were good," I say.

"I kind of threw the ball back to her court."

"You did."

She thinks for a while, rolling the tip of the cigarette into a pointed ash.

"That thing about the sound of the smoke, ooh that was good, that just came to me."

"Mmm."

"You know what it reminded me of?"

"What?" I ask.

"You know, *him*. That's like something he'd say. He could really use the English language. He could manipulate words."

These words themselves manipulate my sleep, the phrases drifting through dreams I can't recall, and the next morning in school when I'm still half-asleep and Mrs. Henmin says of a poet, "He knew how to use the English language," I feel that this is too coincidental not to be momentous. Something compels me to tell others of this coincidence, deprived though

I am of the punch line that would explain its significance. The exact words, after all, have been used within hours to describe my father and a famous poet. But when I tell my best friend Natalie about it, she doesn't even pay attention. She's showing me some photographs she just had developed. "What do you think it means?" I ask.

"This is a really good one of me," she says.

She looks up for my approval and sees me staring at her.

"And you too," she says.

I continue to stare at her.

"I don't know what it means," she says.

In my heart I don't believe that he ever existed, biological necessity to the contrary. Nevertheless, references to my father always intrigue me. Because I have never seen him, not even in photographs, I dream of him in my own version of Braille—odors and shadows, and sounds (usually of a pan being thrown). There's never a face, though often the camera follows a pair of feet. Sometimes there are several pairs of feet. They follow behind me like visible footsteps of invisible men. And although Natalie claims to have prenatal memories (she remembers coming out and being slapped on the bottom), I can go even further: I can feel the temperature, the texture of darkness, and the aroma of my mother's seduction by the lone love of her life. Or so I imagine.

When I arrive home from school, my mother is sitting at the table with Jackie. Jackie always appears about ten minutes after my mother comes home, no matter when she comes. Jackie is like a Geiger counter that can, from a respectable distance, gauge any change in my mother's activities. I'd swear she watches us from her Venetian blinds if her Venetian blinds didn't hang three miles away.

Jackie is the type of person who says things like "Yahoo!" and "Hooray!" when she's happy, but I just think it's playact-

ing because I don't think she's happy. But tell that to her—
she thinks she's the happiest person on earth. When she sees
a good-looking guy (or even a not-so-good-looking guy—let's
put it this way: when she sees a *guy*), she says, "Yum-yum!"
The worst is that my mother laps it right up and even says
it herself. "Yum-yum behind you on your right," she said to
Jackie and me at Burger King the other day. Isn't it obvious to
her that people who say "Yum-yum" and buy unauthorized
biographies and a half-gallon of malted milk balls to eat while
they read them are people who, while they are usually old
and sad themselves, make *you* feel old and sad? And when
she and Jackie laugh together I feel so old and sad I might as
well be stuck in a nursing home with a handicapped toilet as
my only view. What is SO funny? I have to ask, but they can't
answer me: they're laughing too hard.

I walk in just as Jackie is describing a heaviness in her
legs. At first I'm struck with a tentative admiration: however slight, it is at least not my usual disgust. Jackie doesn't
seem like one to admit her shortcomings, and heavy legs is
one of them. She always wears stretch pants that have a strip
of piping sewn down their center to mock a perfect crease.
Under these pants she wears hose, which pulls her thighs into
odd bulges like the lumps from removable football pads. Has
anyone ever looked at her and said, "Yum-yum"?

Then I realize that Jackie is talking about a feeling of heaviness in her legs, not her actual heaviness. It's just the same
old thing again. Jackie thinks my mother is a doctor simply
because my mother works in a doctor's office. She is forever
telling her about her ailments. Then she waits for a diagnosis.
Jackie loves being diagnosed. She thrives on trying to have
diseases.

My mother listens silently during Jackie's long description
of this heaviness. I know that she wants to give me a hug, but
she can't: it would break her concentration. Instead she holds

out her cigarette like a peace pipe, and I take a puff. Then she studies the cigarette while she listens, tapping and rolling its ash to a point. Finally she poses several questions. This is the part Jackie loves best.

"Is this heaviness painful?" my mother asks.

"No, it's not real painful. It's more like a heaviness. But sometimes . . . I mean, sometimes it seems to hurt."

"But it's more a feeling of numbness?"

"Yeah, numbness."

"Is there a lack of sensation when you touch it?" My mother moves closer to her. "Look over there for a second. How many fingers am I touching you with?"

"Two," Jackie says.

"How about now?"

"Oh boy, I don't know. Feels like one. I couldn't really say."

My mother leans back and takes a quick tug at her cigarette and then crushes it in the tray. Jackie watches all of this with rapt and curious eyes. My mother trails her finger around the lip of the ashtray and lets it linger in the groove.

"What did it mean that I couldn't tell how many fingers?"

My mother shakes her head to curtail any talk. She's thinking.

"Ooh, sorry," Jackie whispers.

"Does the numbness radiate outward?" my mother finally asks.

"It seems to."

"How? Does it move in a progression—from here to here to here? Or does it sprout up in different parts of your body?"

"It sprouts up," Jackie says.

My mother lights another cigarette at the stove. She takes down a third cup from the cupboard and pours us coffee. "There are a couple of things that come to mind," she says to Jackie. "But what I would do is wait a few days and see if it's better or worse."

"What if it's the same?"

"Or the same."

"What if it is?"

My mother inhales and lets the smoke fork slowly out of her nose. It's another sign that she's thinking.

"What are the couple of things that come to mind?" Jackie asks.

My mother pours boiling water into a pan of lime Jell-O mix. "Varicose veins." She slices up a banana and drops the slices one by one off the edge of her knife. "Toxic shock syndrome," she says after the first slice plops heavily to the bottom and then fights its way to a floating position. In a few seconds there's a whole layer of baby yellow lifebuoys. When the Jell-O hardens, they'll sink like lead. "Multiple sclerosis," she says at last.

"Multiple sclerosis," Jackie whispers. "Wow." She is ecstatic.

Between Jackie and Sue, I'm about to go crazy. At least Jackie likes me all right, but Sue hates my guts. She despises my mother too. We're not so fond of her either, but it's not the main thing in our lives. Now we have another problem with her: she's left the night shift at the restaurant and become manager of the day shift. The only reason we've been able to live with her so far is that we never see her. Now we have her all evening long. She sits in the living room and sniffs the air for trouble with that nervous, upturned nose of hers.

At least I have an hour to myself after school. Thank God for small favors. But then Sue comes home. She immediately pours herself a Beefeater martini because she thinks it's sophisticated. After one or two drinks she puts a Weight Watchers TV dinner in the oven and drinks white wine while she waits. While she waits she usually accuses me of watering her gin. "Let me smell your breath," she says if she's had a drink too many.

When she finishes eating, she rinses out the foil dish with the water on full blast for as long as it would take someone else to wash a sinkful of dishes, and then fills it with cat food and gives it to her cat. She doesn't think cats should get addicted to human leavings, but neither does she think cats should be humiliated with animal bowls for their food. Frustrated as she is with no boyfriends, this becomes very important and gets mixed up with moral issues like sex, and suddenly she can become vehement and essentially hysterical about why cats should not lick Weight Watchers lasagna. Afterwards she sinks back with a calm exhaustion and there is a slight smile on her face. We hate the cat almost as much as we hate her.

After the cat finishes eating, Sue rinses out the foil again, and after she's done this she just throws it away. Next she scrubs the sink with Soft Scrub, rinses it, and takes a paper towel and wipes away the beads of water. The sink is completely dry and shiny as a mirror. It says, "Please don't turn the water on me." When I turn on the water, Sue jumps visibly in the chair and her nostrils flare. "I'm sorry," I say.

"Don't be sorry," my mother warns.

Sue sips her wine and watches me. I go to the downstairs bathroom, but I know she can hear me. I run the faucet. When I come out, Sue smiles meanly. "Nice way to run up the water bill," she says.

"You should talk," my mother says. "That cat uses up more water than any human being." Sue's cat is named Shiva after the Hindu god of destruction. Behind her back we call Sue "The Goddess of Destruction" and we call her cat "Shitva" after the Hindu god of kitty litter. For days Sue has been worrying about whether she should get Shiva spayed. She says "spaded." She talks about it constantly when she isn't talking about Richard, her old boyfriend, or how youthful she looks for her age, at which point she gives my mother smug, accusatory glances. She talks in a high elated voice that is still oddly normal. It reminds me of someone on stage who has to exaggerate their voice and inflections and still sound ordinary.

It's the fifth day of Sue's new shift. She comes home bright and early. After drying the sink again with a paper towel and pouring a second glass of wine, she starts on her same three subjects. First, the cat. "I found out something *very* interesting today," she says in that theatrical voice. "Somebody told me that the male cat ejaculates within ten seconds of entering the female. The female *then* turns around *quite* often to claw the male. And I said, 'NO WONDER! NO WONDER!'" At this point she throws out both arms in a wide expanse and I get the feeling that she never got over being the lead in the high school play. "*I'd* turn on a man who ejaculated in ten seconds too!"

Ejaculation leads easily into her second subject, Richard. "No one has ever felt the heartache I feel. I feel as if my heart is ripping in two right inside my chest—right inside, *ripping*. I need someone to hold me so I won't—*literally*—break apart. I *know* no one has ever felt this kind of heartache or everyone would be dead. I don't know how I'm still alive," she says.

"I don't know either," my mother responds in her quiet therapist's voice. She looks at Sue and aims slow jets of smoke her way.

This angers Sue and thus leads easily into the third topic: her youthfulness versus my mother's. "I don't know why men call you and they don't call me. I look so much younger. It must be that I don't look like an easy lay."

My mother calmly exhales a wad of smoke and says, "Or maybe you look too easy."

"I seriously doubt that," Sue says with a harsh laugh.

"I guess you're right," my mother says without a hint of sarcasm. It completely rattles Sue, who is gearing up. Her nose, darting the air for a fight, turns red at the tip and white at the bridge. We ignore her.

In bed that night my mother has a good laugh as she searches through her *Thirty Days to a Better Vocabulary*. "That Sue," she pronounces, "is a neurasthenic asshole. Sorry, baby. Had to say it." She stuffs her pillow under her stomach and returns to her vocabulary.

Whenever she takes a drag of her cigarette she turns her head to the side, as if she's being considerate of the book, and blows the smoke into nonoccupied space. The book, since it's a paperback, won't stay open. She turns it over and jerks it backward, but she only succeeds in breaking the binding. True, the book now lies obediently open, but groups of pages drop out and each page, as she turns it, goes its individual way. The edge of mucilage grows wider as each page glides off. "Ah muchacho chiquita muchachos!" she shrieks in disgust. She thinks she is swearing in Spanish. "Chiquita!" she yells again. She thinks "chiquita" means "shit."

But now she sees the humor in it all. She strips off the mucilage like it's a Band-Aid and throws the loose pages in the air. Then she yanks the pillow from under her stomach and flings it on top of me. "Want to play '30 Day Pickup'?" Her laughter breaks into crackles of phlegm: the harder she laughs, the more she has to cough in the end. "Well," she says, "there goes my thirty days to a better vocabulary."

"Unh-hunh . . ."

"But I got a few good words out of it. Today, for instance, they made me wait so long at the bank I was going to be late for my next appointment, so I butted in at the front and said, 'This is a temporal matter!' Nobody said a word, they let me right in." She hits me with the pillow when I don't respond. "So what do you think?" she asks. She hits me again. "Why won't you answer me?"

"It's a temporal reason," I say.

"I love it," she says.

She gets distracted by the sleeveless nightgown which has slipped from her shoulder. Her chin compresses into itself as she tries to see the top of her shoulder. "Can you still see where my swimsuit strap was?"

"No."

"Chiquita. I'm all pale."

"You're still dark."

"Well . . ." she says, as if still thinking about her tan. "I think they're talking in the office like maybe I could start giving some shots."

"I thought you had to be a nurse," I say.

She shrugs. "They're talking about what a great job I do."

"Well, good."

"You think my legs look okay?"

"What are you talking about?"

"You know, OKAY. You know what I mean."

"You know they look okay so don't ask me."

"My stomach's starting to stick out though. Look."

My mother is the envy of all her friends because she's thin. But to me she doesn't look good. She looks too thin. Her collarbones protrude like a clothes hanger. On good days, when she has slept and eaten healthily, she has the angular features of a model, though still perhaps trimmed a little too sharply. On bad days her face is unrelenting in its thinness. On these days it makes me sad just to look at her. What wrinkles, I wonder, were plowed at my birth?

"I think I'll do twenty sit-ups every night," she says. "For a whole week."

Kindled by the doctor's praise and by Jackie's psychosomatic idolatry, my mother buys a white business suit that bears a definite resemblance to a doctor's uniform. That night, when I am startled from a deep sleep by Sue's shrieking ("For crying out loud! Can't I get a little peace in this world!"), I bolt upright in bed and call "Mom!" in a quick jerk of breath. But her bed is empty. It shocks me, and when I turn to see her skeleton hanging in the closet, I scream. My heart rushes in violent waves toward my throat: it is her white suit hanging on the bones of a clothes hanger.

The next day I tell Natalie about it. "So?" she says. "It probably looks nice on her."

"Thank you for just missing the point."

"Oh God, you're so argumentative."

"Okay, just forget it," I say.

"Fine with me." Natalie is a staunch supporter of my mother. If it weren't for the fact that she is black, people would probably mistake them for mother and daughter. Their relationship blossomed during our sophomore year when both of us went through a traumatic event: one day Natalie and I discovered our French teacher, Mrs. Lefebvre, dead on the floor. We had come in during lunch to do her bulletin board. There she was, flopped on the tile like a fish. Her eyes and mouth were open. She had choked to death on her turkey sandwich. It was the second day after Thanksgiving vacation.

Natalie went into shock and they had to take both her and Mrs. Lefebvre to the hospital. As far as I know, I've had no serious psychological repercussions from this event, but its consequence for Natalie was severe. She became so afraid of choking that she became afraid of eating. It wasn't that she didn't want to eat. She wanted to eat, but she was afraid to. I had to sit with her at lunch with my hands poised in the air. This was what I called the "Heimlich Ready Position." It was mortifying to Natalie to think that others might see her in this incapacitated condition (she was always very popular and bright), so she elected me as the only one privy to her humiliation. After all, I saw her go into shock, and if she had had someone else help her through that time, there would have been two people who had seen her helpless and two people, therefore, who had claim to a certain superiority over her. Besides, I don't think anyone else would have gone to all the trouble more than a couple of weeks, not even the Rondettes, who are her second-best friends.

The Rondettes are three black girls who, I must admit, make the drill team come alive. They are forever practicing their soul drills right in the hall. They look like very funky robots clapping once, saluting once, bending once, over and over again, all to a rhythmic chant. If they've got a crowd around them, they'll make the chant obscene. The white students love it more than the blacks. I don't really like the Rondettes, but I guess I'm the only one. Natalie's crazy about them. Whenever she's with them, her accent changes and she starts talking black. All of a sudden everything is "girl" this and "girl" that. Whenever she does this, I hate it.

The Rondettes were nice enough to Natalie during her trouble, but they weren't about to give up their lunch hours for her. The Rondettes are busy people. So it was left up to me to protect Natalie from choking. My mother helped too. Very calmly, she demonstrated the Heimlich maneuver to Natalie, explaining that no matter what went down, even turkey, it would come back up. She taught me the Heimlich maneuver too, and the three of us used to spend hours practicing it on each other. During these times Natalie would lose that skein of nervousness that always enclothed her, even when she was still (she was motionless like an animal sensing danger). My mother, bless her heart, would soothe Natalie and even make her laugh—she was the only one who could. Consequently, Natalie became dependent on my mother, and in some ways they're more like mother and daughter than we are.

On Saturday Natalie comes over and we get ready for the pool in our apartment complex. Sue becomes somewhat hysterical when she sees us. Someone has put water in Shiva's water bowl without rinsing it first. Two briquettes of cat food float about like pieces of poop, and Shiva refuses to drink it. So would I. "Whoever did this should clean it out," Sue says. When neither Natalie or I make a move, she screams, "*Dehydrated!* Do I make myself clear?"

I kind of nod.

"Do I?"

"Yes!" Natalie says quickly.

Now the two briquettes are starting to disperse in the water like brown tablets of Alka-Seltzer. Sue picks up the plastic bowl and slams it into the sink. "Cats are people too!" she screams. "They deserve a little respect! A little love! For God's sake, where's all the love in this world!" She pours herself some wine, pounds the cushions of her chair before sitting down, and glares at us.

Natalie and I dare not say a word or even look at each other.

"You're just like your mother," she hisses. It's supposed to be the ultimate insult.

"Let's leave my mother out of this," I say.

Sue takes another sip and stares into her drink. "You're a little piece of chiquita, as your mother would say."

Natalie and I glance at each other and then back at the floor.

"Yeah, I see you looking at each other. You're a little piece of shit, as I would say. Me, that's who. Me me me." She begins singing a little tune with "me me me" as the only lyrics.

"Let's go," Natalie whispers to me.

"Wait," I mouth back.

In another minute Sue sinks back into her chair in a refreshed stupor, a smile of exhaustion on her face. Her nostrils are dilated; I can see them from across the room.

"See what I mean?" I whisper to Natalie.

My mother comes home immediately after this. I see that she's wearing her new white suit and that she has the collar of her blouse turned stylishly up. Because she looks nice, the collar part makes me both sad and happy, the way I feel when a timid fat girl tries on a new skirt and smooths out her hips. I'm happy when I catch the girl's smile in the mirror because I can't bear to think of the alternative. My mother is starting to affect me this way though I don't know why.

"Girl, you look sharp in that suit!" Natalie exclaims as soon as she sees her.

My mother has a smile on her face. "Really?"

"She thinks she looks like a doctor," Sue says sarcastically from her chair in the corner. She's on her second or third glass of wine.

"Girl, you *do* look like a doctor."

My mother doesn't say anything, but she makes eye contact with me and grins.

Natalie presents her with a photograph of herself and me.

"What a picture of you two," my mother says. "I'm going to put this up in my office."

"What office?" Sue says.

"Natalie looks gorgeous."

"No, I don't."

"Tell the truth, Natalie."

"Well . . ."

My mother laughs and grabs Natalie in a hug. "How you feeling, girl?" she whispers.

Natalie looks at the floor, suddenly shy. "Fine."

My mother squeezes her shoulder again before letting her go. "Everybody ready for a swim?"

We lug ice, a six-pack of Diet Pepsi, chips, a couple of paperbacks, suntan oil, and towels to the pool.

"You're playing Russian roulette with skin cancer," Sue yells to us as we leave.

"God, I wish she'd dig a hole and crawl in," my mother says. She takes a seat in a chaise longue with her book. She oils up until she shines like a body builder. By the end of the summer her face will be wet leather stretched over a skull.

"Is that book good?" Natalie asks.

"No, but it's nasty. Ha ha, just kidding, girls." My mother steps off the chaise longue, which is divided in thirds, and arranges the parts so that they all click level like a bed. Then she turns over and lies on her stomach, head peering over the edge. The pose looks so familiar. It's how she lies in bed. I feel that same sadness as before. For some reason, when I see inconsequential things repeat themselves with her, moods or gestures circling the air above her, I get that feeling again, sad. Too sad, like when I cry at a song about breaking up when I've never in my life broken up. I watch my mother, stretched out, happy head up to view the sights, and I feel my eyes stinging.

"God, what is your problem?" Natalie says in disgust.

"Nothing."

"Don't start doing this now," she says.

"This is the life," my mother says. She deposits her ashtray, a foil disposable from Sue's restaurant, under the lounge chair. When she reaches for her cigarette, her arm wraps around the side of the chair and feels blindly along the cement. "Would you rub some stuff on my back, baby? Thanks." She lifts her head up like she's doing the breaststroke (it's as close as she'll get to swimming) and exhales some smoke. She checks her straps for a tan and then aligns her forearm with Natalie's. "Girl, you be dark as me," she says with her hoarse laugh.

"Girl, I wish I was that thin," Natalie says.

I can't believe it. Here I am putting oil on my mother and she's talking black and Natalie is talking black back to her. "Thanks a lot," I say.

"You're welcome for whatever it was," Natalie says.

My mother laughs and feels on the cement for her cigarette. I rub the lotion on her back until it shines. Then I move over to Natalie, whose complexion contrasts so sharply. My mother's tanned skin becomes thinly webbed with light creases as it thickens and puckers from the heat, but Natalie's skin grows into rich cherry wood with a gloss of burgundy shining on her shoulders.

"You're so lucky you don't get freckles," I say.

"I'm so lucky," Natalie says.

"So shut up," I say.

"Here, I'll put some on you."

"I'm going in. Aren't you going in?"

"I'm having a drink first."

"Natalie?"

"What?"

I flick at something on my thigh. When I look down, I discover it was a firefly. Why was it out during the day? On my leg is a fluorescent smudge.

"What?"

"Ooh," I say. "Look at that."

"Wha-aat?"

"Natalie?"

"What!"

"How come you don't ever talk black to me?"

"What are you talking about?"

"You talk black to the Rondettes, *and to my mother.* But not to me."

"Yes I do."

"You never call me 'girl.' "

"Yes I do."

"No you don't."

"Shut up," Natalie says.

"You like them more than me."

"God, who wouldn't the way you act."

"I'm serious," I say. "I mean it."

Natalie looks away and I see her jaw drop. I turn to see, oh please no, it's Jackie in a yellow bathing suit fringed with a little yellow skirt. Perfect for a dancing pink pig. Her legs shoot upward like giant sugar cones. They start out skinny but make up for it at the top.

"Hi, Jackie," my mother says dreamily. Her arms are spread out limply to catch the sun. On the cement her hands curl inward, palms up, as if she's doing the dog paddle.

When Jackie sits down, her butt appears below the chair, striped in green vinyl. "Yum-yum on your left."

"Definitely," my mother murmurs.

"Smack smack."

"Mmm."

"Not to change the subject," I interrupt, "but is ANYBODY going in the pool?"

"I would but my foot hurts," Jackie says.

"What's wrong?" my mother asks.

"A radiating pain."

"Another one?" I say.

"Where?"

"Right here in the center of my foot."

"Could be a plantar's wart," my mother says. "Is it a surface pain or does it have a core?" I jump in before I can hear anything else. I swim until I'm in the deep end where the ladder descends as deeply as the water. I follow it down and with the blue water surrounding me like umbilical fluid and my hair alive as Medusa's I look at the submerged bottommost rung and think, There she is—that's what she used to be like. The water is very cold. I'm shivering when I come up for air.

On Tuesday, with a week left of school, we have our final examinations. At the lockers before the English exam someone shows me the latest issue of the school newspaper. One of the senior profiles is of Natalie, but the photograph is horrible. At the time Natalie offered the school photographer one of her own pictures, but he shouldered her up against the window, turned the camera vertically, and snapped. Even I know that when you take pictures against the light, white people come out black and black people come out silhouettes. Poor Natalie's finely featured ebony is a featureless glob of newsprint ink; the light shafting through her hair has turned her processed strands into snakes.

I grab the newspaper and hide it. If she sees this before the exam, she'll fail for sure. As I take my seat behind her I can't help but marvel at what a good friend I am. It's those little things I do that should clue in more people than—oh well—they do.

Mrs. Henmin has warned us beforehand that if we write "Wadsworth" for "Wordsworth" we get an automatic *F*. I write: "I think this shows a negative attitude because you're assuming the worst. If I showed you a picture of half a glass of water, would you give me an automatic *F* if I said it was half full just because you assumed the worst and thought it was half empty? Sorry, but I just thought I should express my honest opinion."

Without thinking I tap Natalie on the shoulder and show her what I've written. She nods in approval and goes back to work. This little conference is treated as naturally as one treats a shoplifter who, with arms too full of a TV, asks the clerk to open the door for him. For once the room is full of quiet students who have done their studying; the usual goof-offs are the ones most frantic to have their say in court. They are nervous and earnest, like freshly shaved hoodlums before the judge.

I can hear the air currents from the vents, but the air remains thick with the hot dreaminess of a schoolday in summer. The slam of a door down the hall echoes a world we have left. I am losing my concentration.

When I come to a question about reincarnation and what poems illustrate it and how and why do I think that (please be specific), I can't remember. The answer gnaws at me like a forgotten previous life. I can't help but think how appropriate this is, more appropriate in fact than if I had simply known the answer—had simply led a single life—and so I write down this observation instead of the answer. When I finish, I drop my pen and exercise my fingers. I do in fact feel I've led several lives, I just don't know what they are or where they went. My father, I am sure, has not only led many lives, he's created many. A terrible thought occurs to me: my mother and I are just one of his many. Was he just one of her many? I decide to press her for the answer, to find out what really happened. She's always been vague about the subject. An even worse thought occurs: suppose she doesn't even remember?

I can hardly cope with this possibility. I light a cigarette and blow the smoke hard toward the ceiling. The newly demure rowdies don't dare draw attention to me. But it wouldn't matter. I don't really notice what I'm doing. Neither does Mrs. Henmin. She is staring out the window. That funny looking body of hers heaves in sighs or dreams. As she stares outside, her overlooked face deepens with sadness. Her stomach, which she so often grabs like a good luck charm, no longer seems set at that jaunty angle suitable for our laughs. It sags. She continues to look out the window, oblivious to the fact that I'm smoking. In fact, she herself has slipped a cigarette out of her purse. We are both, I seem to understand, thinking back to the same time. For Mrs. Henmin it didn't happen; for my mother it did. I make a mental note not to repeat either mistake.

Still at the window, Mrs. Henmin smokes the cigarette only so long as she needs it for her thoughts, stubs it out on the pane, and throws it outside. Furrowed student foreheads pop up like toast to witness this miracle. That bit of ash on the window squats more proudly than any of the bits of knowledge she has given us. It's probably the only thing we'll remember about her in a few years.

That afternoon I have a brief reign as a celebrity. Three

or four boys tell me they would have asked me out if they'd known how I really was. It's too late now. I try not to look back with regrets, but why all these years did I confine my smoking to the toilet? Mrs. Henmin and I have come out of the closet, but the room is emptying in one week. Still, I am easily gratified.

"It's not too late, you can date them over the summer," my mother tells me.

"It's too late," I say. "So forget it."

"Here." She shakes up a cigarette from her pack.

"No, I've given up smoking."

"But I just bought that Topol toothpaste. It takes out nicotine stains if that's what you're worried about."

"No."

"Oh. Well, I'm not going to smoke if you're not."

"Go ahead."

"No. Not if you don't," she says sadly. She places the cigarette in the flat of her palm and looks down at it. Her pet fag that's died.

"All right, give it to me," I say.

We're sitting at a restaurant where she's taken me to celebrate my graduation. It's a restaurant above our means and I have the feeling that the waiters, the customers, the dishwashers—everybody—has immediately sensed this. We catch ourselves gawking as a waiter opens a bottle of wine at the table next to us and hands the cork to the oldest man, whose white hair, at each temple, has receded in finely speckled triangles. He breathes in the darkened cork with his eyes closed.

"Do you wish they were your parents?" my mother asks me.

"They're too old."

"You know what I mean."

"If they were younger, yes. Definitely yes," I say.

"I love it," she says. Then she calls the waiter and orders a bottle of house wine. She nods at me. "Two can play this game."

"You'll probably have to drink it alone, you know."

"Don't worry. You're grown up. Oh my God, I can't believe it: my little baby, all grown up."

The waiter opens the bottle in front of us and she smells the cork. "Mm-hmm, very nice," she says. He pours two glasses and she winks at me. "See? Here's to your graduation."

"Thanks. You drink both of them." Now I'll get her drunk and then I'll pop the question. Oh God, like father like daughter.

"You know what?" she says and puts her chin into her palm.

"What?"

She pivots her head both ways to make sure no one is listening. "I'm going to cry at your graduation."

"Why?"

"I don't know."

"I'm not."

"Well you're maybe not. But I am. Cause you're leaving me . . ." she says.

"I'm not leaving you."

"Yes you are."

"Just to go to school is all."

"That's enough."

"Don't say that. Now I'll feel guilty."

"Don't feel guilty," she says. And then, after exhaling, "Just don't go."

"Mom!"

"I can't help it. I'm going to cry if you go."

I look at her with my mouth open to speak, yet I don't know what to say. Because my mouth is open, she is confused for a second and thinks I'm the one who has cried out. But it's come from the table next to us. The delicate liver spots on the temples of the white-haired man have turned a flaming pink. His eyes and mouth are wide and round.

"Chiquita!" my mother whispers.

"Is there a doctor in the house?" the wife screams. My

mother immediately stands up. She walks calmly over to the man, and in the midst of uselessly gesticulating people she grabs him from behind in the Heimlich maneuver and pops her fist against his diaphragm. She has saved a life. She really has. And she is wearing her white suit.

When she winks and gives me the thumbs-up sign, all action stops. Everyone turns to stare silently at me.

MEETING

IN

TOKYO

During a business trip to Tokyo I engaged one of the secretaries in a conversation about curry. I was up from my home in Kyushu, but I let it be known I knew my way around this overwhelming city. "Let's take the subway to Akasaka and have curry at that Indian restaurant," I suggested. I had to cough before mentioning its name. But she knew what I meant. She accepted and that was that.

From the Indian restaurant we slipped by taxi to Shinjuku, where the lights and noise were even more excessive. We wove through the crowds until I found a coffee shop I liked. It bordered the blue cinema district, and during our conversation the distant catcalls from porno revues scratched at the edge of our voices.

It was through this seedy district that we strolled on the way to her train station. Giant billboards rose above the theaters and illustrated pivotal scenes from this movie and that. Beyond them, lights of hotels blinked purple and red and I made a move to hold her hand.

At the Seibu Shinjuku station I bought a ticket in order to escort her up the stairs, and possibly farther. We barely made it. The warning whistle suddenly blew, the doors swished open, and she stepped inside the train without me. As the second whistle sounded, I reached in and pulled her out just as the doors were sealing shut. I guided her down the stairs and back out into the theater district. My hand at the small of her back met pressure but no resistance as I guided her up the hill toward the colorful hotels. From the Pachinko parlors came the metal waterfalls of victory. Afterwards I made sure she boarded the final train at 12:08. I attempted a brisk businesslike wave, then returned to the coffee shop we had sat in earlier and thought about what I'd done.

I had to confess some forethought in selecting a coffee shop where the clangor of flesh-peddling and Pachinko games could brush against our privacy with disconcerting sensations. But the rest was accidental. That she caught her train at Seibu Shinjuku in the middle of the cinema district, thereby requiring a visual romp through scenes of torture and sodomy, was simply a stroke of good fortune. And although the audacious timing of pulling her through the doors between the two whistle blasts had secured the seduction, this flamboyance was no more than my sudden desire not to make the long commute to her apartment.

During our brief passionate struggle, she called out my name. "Mister Naoka!" she cried. I admired her skillful secretarial juggling between abandon and deference, but when another wanton outburst came addressed in the honorific, I couldn't hold back at the comedy. I burst into a laugh, although I managed quickly to disguise it as my orgasm. Wouldn't my old friend Ashida like to see the honorable Mister Naoka now? I chuckled to myself, but my amusement flickered to sadness at the thought of my lost companion. This secretary I was with, attempting to bluff me with outlandish gyrations, never realized that she herself had been faked out.

As I sat alone in the coffee shop, the same waiter who had served us earlier took my order. He arranged a clean ashtray on the otherwise empty table, and in front of that placed a hot towel. I ordered Coffee Kilimanjaro. From behind the bar the steward took the order and commenced his operations with the affected strokes of a bartender. A line of coffee beakers was displayed before him like glass barbells. He undid one of the barbells and poured boiling water into the lower bulb. The flow of water grew long and dramatic as he lifted the kettle higher. At the instant he cocked the kettle to stop the flow he looked up at me with the hint of a smile. As if to flaunt the perfect precision of his movements, he wore white gloves.

The pleasure with which I viewed his refined movements recalled my own theatrical precision in hauling the secretary through the closing doors of her train. Were I to repeat the action, it would be all the more pleasurable for its added calculation. A military step properly performed is, after all, the most pleasurable to watch, despite its endless repetition.

I settled into my seat. Although the coffee shop was fairly large, each setting was cramped. The low easy chair forced me into an unnatural delicacy by springing my knees against the underside of the table. If I leaned back comfortably, which the cushions encouraged me to do, my legs jacked the table in the air. It recalled a memory. One evening early in my career I was called upon to dine with some American businessmen. When we sat down on the floor to eat, my crossed legs sprang up like crowbars and dug into the Americans sitting next to me. My Japanese companions swelled with pride at my uncontained lankiness. I stood a head taller than these Americans who, like me, must also have been chosen partly because of their (obversely) accommodating sizes: they were all short. During the meal their fingers kept searching out the handles of their emptied coffee cups. Ah, I surmised. "Refills!" I called over in Japanese. Then I switched to English. "Let's have more coffee," I said in a friendly way.

I sipped on my Kilimanjaro and remembered the episode. It was ten years ago, at the beginning of my career. I was living in Tokyo and felt Armageddon all around me and fancied myself suicidally carefree. In my mind I was constantly describing how I must appear to others: So tall . . . So confident . . . There's nothing he won't do . . . I wish I were like him . . . During these early business dinners with Americans, such descriptions of myself swam through my head. As I plowed right into Western-style meals with my fork, I almost had to keep myself from laughing out loud.

The Americans and I finished our food in sync while across from us my Japanese co-workers and superiors were hardly halfway through the torturous process of eating European-style, tidbits of rice nudged precariously onto the backs of forks and doomed to slip off before reaching any mouths. When they noticed they were lagging far behind the Americans, they simply ended their meals and went hungry rather than risk possible impoliteness. But when we all ate Japanese-style, the tables were turned. My co-workers practically swallowed their bowl of rice in a single gulp while the Americans became the dainty ones who clenched lower and lower on their chopsticks until they were clamping onto their food with a pincer movement of fingers rather than sticks. Again I somehow managed to time my eating to suit these Americans twiddling over their food like crabs.

My co-workers asked me why the Americans seemed to like me. I said it was because when I saw food before me I ate it. I forgot where I was or how I should behave. I just grabbed the fork and got up the rice the best way I could. "You should do the same," I suggested, but I knew they wouldn't. They had to follow the lead of our superiors who sat across the table trying to coax loose vegetables onto an upside-down fork. Sometimes their efforts were so futile it was nerve-wracking to the extreme. Across the table their shaking hands were all that I could see. My focus grew so intent that when I looked up from their trembling fingers I expected to find my friend Ashida, my lost friend Ashida, his nervous shaking hands, the cigarette bobbing up and down. The things I would then think about my superiors . . . I had a lack of respect for them for which I alternately praised and berated myself. Though I

still obeyed the multiple conventions of work hierarchy and
social etiquette, I liked to think that a sheen of slick weariness
separated my own conformity from the others' and proved
attractive to the American customers simply through its un-
expectedness.

Around this time, when I was still living in Tokyo, an
American began working in our office and I observed him.
His name was Sandy. As he was taken around and introduced
to everyone, he showed us each his styrofoam cup with a
7-Eleven logo on it. He seemed extremely amused at having
found a 7-Eleven store nearby, and everyone bowed happily,
pleased to have pleased him. By the second day he was practicing behind-the-back bank shots into the wastebasket. He
was still civil enough to return our greetings. "Good morning," I said to him in English as I passed. "How's it going?" he
answered with a casual nod and flipped a wad of paper.

Later, when I asked him a question about English, he looked
up slowly. "Say what, guy?"

I went no further. After carrying the sound of his utterance
back to my desk, I repeated it over and over until it clicked
into three words. I wrote them down. I didn't know what
they meant.

By the end of the week this new American employee began
avoiding us. He retreated to his desk and sat behind it whenever he saw any office workers approaching him with an
inquiry. As they spoke to him, he lowered his head and
went through a disconcerting little ritual. He turned his wrist
inward and fiddled elaborately with his watchband until he
finally unhooked it. Then he spread the watch before him on
the desktop, the bands splayed flat like tortured arms, and
leaned heavily over the watch to check the time. Only then
did he look up to listen.

His questioners immediately bowed, thanked him for his
time, and left before asking him their question.

Throughout the day the quiet of our office was interrupted

by his jarring spells of laughter. When we looked over he would be alone, reading our advertising copy. He had fashioned his laughter into a falsetto wheeze, which was very disturbing.

Although he didn't know any Japanese except isolated words that he sprang on us like karate chops while we stood by with compliments (*Him:* Idiot! Boring! Nice! Idiot! Double idiot! Thanks! Ah so! Well! Uh, like uh! Idiot! *Us:* How superbly you speak!), he made no such concessions when he spoke to us in English.

Him: I wannahaisdahbaahhortheresaprahifyoudahhhtohan bats dayorelse.
Us: Yes, I see.
Then the follow-up later that day.
Him: So whassatory?
Us: Yes, I see.
Him: Kaaa . . . RYSSS! What is wrong with you people?

This last sentence he always spoke slowly and clearly, and each day it would be the only sentence we understood. What is wrong with you people? We slunk away.

One morning I gave him the ad copy I had written: *If you always use it, it will refresh your skin and make smooth. And then unconsciously you will take back healthy and clear skin.* For the rest of the day he whinnied deliriously whenever he looked at it. I couldn't stop hearing his laughter. Even in the rest room, where I entombed myself in a stall, his sour revelry slid under the door and found me. Beneath me the toilet began to shake. Oh. An earthquake. I would go gladly to my death.

No. Just a tremor. I was still alive.

Late in the afternoon Sandy handed my ad copy back to

me and said in a colorless voice, "Yeah, it's perfect." Then he said in Japanese, "Splendid, right!"

By now my embarrassment was so profound that I left work not thinking of his silly attempts at Japanese and how I could ridicule them, but of my own horrible English and the howling of his American friends when he repeated my advertising slogan. The friends would reach into their breast pockets and take out their notebooks to write down another funny example of Japanese English. They would be gathered in a restaurant and their happy derision would be loud and public and fueled by beer.

My face burned and perspired. I tapped a folded handkerchief to my upper lip while the other commuters regarded my condition without turning their heads. In the succeeding days I struggled visibly to do better in my job—for some reason I struggled still harder to please this American—and soon thereafter I was transferred to the island of Kyushu where missionaries and potentates had once made their stand but where nothing much happened anymore.

I grappled with the reasons for my transfer to this southern island. I reviewed the advertising campaigns to which I had contributed my efforts. I had done nothing on my own; how could I be at fault? Had I unknowingly perpetrated something like *Snatch*, a new candy bar marketed throughout Hokkaido and readied for Honshu, before someone came forward and explained that the English we were so proud of meant a woman's crotch? I repeated the English phrases I had used, hoping to find in a foreign grammatical structure the personal accountability that didn't exist in my own world. If I was personally at fault, I wanted to know. If I wasn't, I wanted to go somewhere else.

I didn't want to go to Kyushu. For one, it carried the small stain of an unpleasant memory. For another, I had dared to hope for a transfer to the United States. In the U.S. I planned to call on two American girls Ashida and I had met during college. I imagined capturing the casual tone of their life-style and moving easily among several American friends. But the picture was now marred by the loss of Ashida and the introduction of a wife who spoke no English and was country-shy.

After a time, the picture of my sitting at an American bar and talking sports faded. After several years, the snapshot went blank. I was now settled into my job in Kyushu, and a few times each year I traveled to Tokyo. At home I never spoke to my wife. I kept my head down at the dinner table. Sometimes I watched myself with horror as I handed her an empty rice bowl in a peremptory, silent command for her to refill it. What had happened to me? When I came home and she served me tea like an obsequious office girl, I didn't know what to think. She retreated to whatever personal memories her teacup held, and I retreated to mine. It was impossible to sip tea without feeling akin to the myriad other moments in your life when you were doing exactly that: nothing but sipping tea, the insignificant moment held like the eye of a hurricane while life swirled around you. Sometimes the aroma of musk in calligraphy ink affected me in the same way, but the memories it provoked were more exotic and gravid. A teacup rolled about in your hands like a common egg, inert, mundane, the gift of everyday life. Memories inspired by tea were just the things that had happened.

What had happened was that I grew up in a small town near Kanazawa where I attended a public high school and was thus for all practical purposes fated to a college on the second or third tier. Knowing this, my friend Ashida and I worked hard but we didn't kill ourselves. Why stay up half the night, week after week, and nearly ruin our health when the result was as good as foregone? But our teachers didn't see it that way. Each week I heard the squeak of a bicycle and the metal scrape of the kickstand, and in would walk my teacher for his weekly visit. I stood rolling my eyes until my mother pushed me and I shuffled in and bowed. This time it was the new English teacher, Ikeda-sensei.

We took our places on the tatami floor and my mother served tea and bean pastries. Ikeda-sensei introduced himself to my mother and offered his brief autobiography, the schools he had attended including a seminar at the University of Hawaii, as well as his trip to the U.S. and the states he had visited. My mother and I nodded in unison as he listed each state. When he mentioned one we couldn't place, I went in search of a map which we then spread over the table after my mother moved the teapot and cups of tea to the floor beside her. We hunched over the map. Ikeda-sensei's finger landed with a thud. "Idaho!" he pronounced triumphantly. "Hmm!" we exclaimed. "So big!" The states of the U.S. were generously splashed on the map. Our own country was a delicate sliver choked by water, nervously scratched on the atlas by a rapidograph.

We folded the map and my mother brought the tea and pastries back up to the table. She emptied our lukewarm cups and refilled the teapot with hot water from the thermos. She poured the tea almost immediately. Then my teacher began. "Your son is a good boy. Everyone admires his size and strength." My mother smiled. Ikeda-sensei cuffed my shoulder and laughed. "Yes, it's true," he said. "Look at him."

Both my mother and he looked at me and smiled approvingly.

"But he is not working as hard as he possibly can. Each morning he comes to school fresh-faced and apple-cheeked while the other students are pale and wan."

My mother, in her kind voice which rose higher and sweeter as the words grew more polite, explained that she had accepted the fact that I no longer had the credentials which would lead me to a top school. So now the kind of effort which required sleeplessness was for those private high school students who realistically had a shot at a major university.

"Yes," Ikeda-sensei explained, "that is generally true. But only last year we had a student who got into Tokyo University."

"Ohhh!" my mother exclaimed. She nodded appreciatively. Then we all fell silent and looked down. My mother picked up the teapot to refresh Ikeda-sensei's tea, but he declined and pushed his fists against the tatami to hoist himself up.

"Well then," he said, "it's agreed that we'll try harder." He turned to me and bowed. With a catch in his voice he addressed me directly. "I will try harder as your teacher not to let you down." He bowed deeply and sincerely.

I felt very moved by my teacher's declaration, and indeed I felt my mother beside me draw in her breath and hold her mouth tight. I followed Mr. Ikeda outside and stood by his bicycle. He patted my shoulder. "I don't want you to ruin your health. You're growing big and strong, and you need your sleep. But your classmates are working so hard. Can't you work just a little bit harder to show them you appreciate their efforts?" I felt tears come to my eyes. He patted me again. "There, there," he said. Then he pushed off on his bike. Despite a dangerous unsteadiness in his balance, he turned his head and lifted a hand. Even today I see him clearly, waving to me from his wobbling bicycle.

Two years later I was an improved student, and what's more, I was over six feet tall. The now monthly visits from my teacher changed in tone. Most of the conversations revolved around my height. Due to my build I was treated like a star, and I developed an easy confidence with my teachers, who complimented me on my physique. During conferences they treated my height as though it were an obscure area of scholarship. They asked my parents detailed questions:

Was anyone else tall in my family? No one?

What kind of tall behaviorisms did I have as a child?

When did my parents first have an inkling that I would be tall?

What did this inkling feel like?

I hated it when my father had come home early enough from work to be present at these conversations. He embellished insignificant details until they became full-fledged anecdotes. A fondness for round things to stick in my mouth became the mad desire for an American basketball which, being only a year old, I was unable to communicate verbally to my parents. But my father, who had this inkling that I would be tall, figured it out. "I knew it for a certainty," he explained, "when my son desired steak for breakfast." Seated cross-legged on the tatami, he posed his arms atop each knee before delivering the punch line. "That's what American athletes eat," he said.

My teachers appeared just as limber in jumping over the gaps in logic and voicing their approval. "An amazing thing, to want steak for breakfast. He actually said this?" My mother nodded. Gradually, when called upon, she had learned to invent these small details as well as the surge of parental pride she felt upon first noticing them. After one of these conferences she was so embarrassed she said nothing over dinner, and turned on the TV to cover the silence. On the nightly singing show the introduction of Hideki, who was the raging adolescent heartthrob, was preceded by a near-hysterical recitation of his vital statistics, climaxing with his height—183 centimeters. My height exactly.

Oh well, I thought, if all else fails at least I have one thing going for me. Meanwhile, my friend Ashida stayed short. Nobody asked his parents when they first had an inkling that puberty wouldn't affect him. He remained nervous and small, a timorous, innocent hoodlum punished with several weeks of extra mopping duty after the teachers caught him with a cigarette.

I always wondered what the teacher said to Ashida and his parents during his home conferences. One day I asked him. "Ikeda-sensei says I need to be a better student," Ashida said. "Toguchi-sensei says I need to avoid delinquent behavior." He held up his cigarette. "Aso-sensei says I need to be more outgoing. Ito-sensei says I need to maintain my friendship with you through loyalty, more outgoingness, better scholarship, and less delinquent behavior."

"Ito-sensei said that?"

Ashida snickered jumpily and inhaled on the cigarette. He was the nobody I almost was, and after high school we spent two years at a *ronin* preparatory school trying to get into a college. We tried to pretend we were really the masterless samurai the term *ronin* originally meant; after all, the masterless samurais were the ones on TV who got to grow out all their hair, and that's the first thing we started to do after getting out of high school. Ashida grew his hair long and unkempt and refused to have it trimmed at all. Split ends eventually layered it until it swung in the air like a grass skirt. My own hair was bushy and grew over me like a black rain cloud. Seen together, we were an ugly sight. We were warriors in search of a master.

We comforted ourselves by listening to the albums of Inoue Yosui, our favorite singer. On the inside jacket of one of his albums Yosui had charted his personal history on a graph. Small photographs punctuated significant events, and there he was in high school, short-haired and severe in his black military uniform. At one-year intervals after the high school photograph, intersection after intersection on the graph recorded this notation:

Took entrance exam.

Failed.

But Yosui learned integrity from failure and became a famous musician who refused to appear on TV. Likewise, we planned to learn integrity from our failure and thereby avoid becoming company men (although we planned to accept any TV offers that came our way). Like us, Yosui came from a small village and often wrote nostalgically of his hometown. There is a famous saying: The farther you are from your hometown the more nostalgic you become about it. We projected a nostalgia for our hometown through our desire to escape from it.

After two years of *ronin* we were both accepted at a mediocre college near Tokyo. Our life burst with freedom and leisure. For the first three years, armed with Yosui albums, we watched with equanimity the nearly insane April rush of new graduates swarming Tokyo for jobs. During the summers, coddled by parents who had already divined our busy future as company men, we were free to do as we wished.

One of these summers, during a trip to Kyushu, we actually passed through the town where I now live. We met a woman on the train and innocently fell into conversation with her. She appeared to be quite sane until well into her chatter. Suddenly all that changed. She began to tell us something, but her own spurt of laughter cut her off. When she recovered, she started again. During the war, she said, her brother died in the A-bomb explosion while she was riding her bicycle beyond the epicenter. I nodded, more out of wariness than sympathy. To this day, she continued, she wondered whether he exploded or disintegrated. Upon saying this, she dissolved into a crazy cackling, and to my shock, Ashida joined her. Together they laughed like hyenas, a maniacal lethal siren, while I sat soberly and stared at them.

Finally she stopped long enough to tell us that she was going to set herself on fire to find out the real story. "Then I'll know!" Her mouth blew open to release more dammed-up snorting. Beside me, through the spasms of his laughter, I could see Ashida trembling. Since I was hardly amused at any of this, the woman turned on me and began to taunt my seriousness. She invited Ashida to join in. Ashida indicated approval with fluttering nods and groped for a cigarette that immediately flew out of his nervous hands like a comedic prop. Then the woman dismissed us both with loud insults and stood up to move to another seat. No one on the rest of the train acknowledged that any of this was happening, so as the woman searched for another seat she hurled personalized commands to each of the other passengers who were ignoring her.

"Take off your hat!" she barked to this one.

"Take out your teeth and look at them!" to another one.

"Take off your hair and use it as a wallet!" she commanded a poor elderly man with a black toupee.

With each insult she stood by their side and waited for a reaction. There was none. The woman cackled louder and louder at their neutral masks and feigned deafness. This isn't laughter, I remember thinking, it's something else but I don't know what.

A few years later I heard it again. The same kind of malicious stage laughter emanated from Sandy, the new American employee, as he sat at his desk while each morning our female office workers ceremoniously served him tea and he ignored them, preferring to bring in coffee from the 7-Eleven store. Each morning he drank the coffee in great fits of hilarity while a confusing cloud of nostalgia engulfed me. His laughter billowed throughout the office in high-pitched convulsions; it continued daily and people were afraid to ask the joke. When he was on the phone engaged in loud and shameless personal conversation, our heads were turned and studious. He erupted in a braying that dared us to eavesdrop and mocked us for the attempt to understand his English. Indeed, it seemed to me, this laughter sloshing about his upper registers was an excess of spit. Soon he would scuttle away like a cockroach, emerging later from other Far Eastern cracks when he sniffed gullibility nearby.

And yet I had redoubled my efforts to please this person. I knew things were going downhill when I found myself reddening uncontrollably at the thought of him mocking the advertising copy I had submitted. *If you always use it, it will refresh your skin and make smooth. And then unconsciously you will take back healthy and clear skin.* What was so bad about it? I was determined to ask.

I waited until he was away from his desk so he couldn't perform his ritual with the wristwatch. Then I went up to him with the ad copy he had snorted at but not corrected. As I began my carefully rehearsed first sentence, the American removed his thick college ring and began polishing it against his shirt as though it were an apple. He polished and polished, studied it, and then polished it some more. Then he took out his shirttail and screwed it back and forth through the ring. He blew on it and slipped it back on his finger.

Finally he looked at me. "*Omai!*" he exclaimed with exasperation, addressing me with the crudest form of "you." Instinctively I jumped back at the language he had used, just as he must have known I would, and instantly I knew I had lost.

"Thank you very much," I slurred quickly in English. To my disgust I found myself bowing and scurrying away. I sat at my desk, heaving. Unaccountably, the image of my teacher atop his bicycle swelled before me. I felt the beginning of tears. What had happened to me? How had I come to this? Perhaps I had only climbed a single step each week, but each week I had climbed imperceptibly higher. Suddenly I had accepted the stakes; when I looked down, the stakes were too high.

I waved my arm at the waiter and he hurried to my table with the check. I was the only one left in the coffee shop. I could sense that the waiter and steward wanted to shut down and go home. "Another cup of coffee," I said.

A flicker of perturbation crossed the waiter's face as he

readied himself to protest. After a second's pause, he bowed. "Coffee Kilimanjaro correct, sir?"

"Yes," I said.

The steward, beginning to slump on his stool, jerked to alertness and began to prepare the coffee. Again I found myself oddly thrilled by the formalized precision of his technique. I remembered the thrill of sweeping the secretary from her train without a second to spare. Again I loved the exact timing of the train attendant's two whistles. Those hurrying up the stairway, upon hearing the first whistle, could decide in an instinctive assessment of distance and footspeed whether or not to make a run for it. They knew the timing of the whistle blasts. They knew the speed of the closing doors. They knew how to hurtle themselves in sideways as the pneumatic jaws were sealing—and hurtle they did, just as I was reaching in and pulling the secretary out. Whatever our varying intentions, wherever our destinations, we had this in common. The beat of time was engraved in everyone's bones. All of us, scurrying strangers, were united by this. I wanted to turn on the stairway and greet the rush as the first whistle sounded. "My friends!" I wanted to shout. "Run!"

And should the attendant ever vary the beat between the two whistle blasts? Should a minute ever decide to be 61 seconds, even for a second? I would have remained faithful to my wife, but mathematics would be lost. Departed friends would return. The world would make no sense.

Wasn't mathematics simply an attempt to explain everything in relation to the perfect circle, which itself needs no explanation? Wasn't there a reason why the Yamanote Line remained the connecting link to all the other trains, going around in one huge circle, the trains never more than a few seconds off? Wasn't there a reason that the bums chose this train for their naps, their dreams hurling round and round, the invisible numbers of their lives swirling into the brief

visible circle of perfection, and, thus refreshed and newly
imbued, could get off where they started?

And wasn't this why Ashida and I had spent an April day
riding and riding the Yamanote Line while our appointments
for job interviews were left behind like straggling passengers
on the platform, a blur in our lives that we chose to ignore?
Ashida claimed it was impossible to commit suicide on this
line: all the pedestrian walkways were guarded by high fences
that curled inward like fingers to prevent them from being
scaled. Neither failure nor suicide were tolerated—putting us,
we joked, in a no-win situation.

But our brief bluster of rebellion ended, and on our last
day in Tokyo Ashida and I went to all our job interviews.
That evening we celebrated with sushi and beer at a cramped,
homey restaurant. From there we walked to Olympic Park
and Ashida, in a burst of euphoria, began to run around
the track. I climbed the pedestrian walkway to watch. How
ironic, I thought, the overpass was unbarricaded, nothing to
prevent me from throwing myself under the churning legs of
a passing runner.

I leaned over the edge to yell at Ashida. I could hear him
coming but could see nothing. Then his figure broke through
the darkness, a visual Doppler effect to his sound. Before I
could focus running sounds to running forms, he passed under
me in a swish, furthering the sensory illusions. I knew he
couldn't be going that fast, but by the time I completed this
thought he was gone. He disappeared for a long while. The
track was huge; a stadium sat in the middle of it and even in
the daytime one couldn't see across it.

In a few minutes Ashida appeared again. He went around
and around, and in the long gaps of his absence I stood in
the stillness and waited for my body to sense when he would
approach again. Beyond my sight and hearing, a breeze was
building. I was filled with a sudden pleasure at the exact way

his dark form moved with the dark that itself seemed to be moving, chasing its sliding monolith until he caught up with it and then surpassed it and only then became visible to the inferior human eye. He ran on and on and my pleasure increased, not because of his competitive pace or the quantity of kilometers he was accumulating, but because of the circle he was completing again and again. In a secret way I longed for a similar motion that would take me from job to home and back again.

When the wave of stillness felt timed to end, I waited for the sound of gravel to kick up. I waited longer. Thinking Ashida might have exhausted himself and was walking back, I extended the rhythm of his absence to its breaking point, but still he didn't come. Finally I climbed down and walked the track myself. I mounted the steps to the stadium's bolted doors and looked around. Then I checked the walkway again, and then called his name. It was hard to say it. The human voice, the voice of reason, was not contained within this circle.

M O R N I N G

A T   T H E

B E A C H

The woman known as Carla stepped outside to go shopping. On Ocean Avenue the neighborhood was instantly aware of her activity. She walked past a cluster of Cuban men who regarded her without acknowledgment and came to the Al Lado Del Mar Hotel, in front of which her car was parked. As she fussed with the windshield shade, she tipped her head toward the aged occupants of Terrace Harbour, out on their chairs.

Carla maneuvered the huge cardboard fan off the windshield and onto the backseat. Protected from the sun, the steering wheel was cool and she sped away like a demon. Between hotels the ocean flipped by in staggered blue windows.

From the patio of Terrace Harbour, Mrs. R. watched her go. She whistled three notes and said, "The sun's already bright." She had a certain code for each neighbor's absence, and was able to relay the information through a creatively phrased message that sometimes incorporated music.

The Terrace Harbour housed mostly elderly residents who were usually able to pay in advance on a monthly basis. It had hung a sign for house painters to keep its aqua exterior cheerful. One of the residents had applied for the job but was turned down.

Like all the hotels along the street, the front porch of Terrace Harbour was furrowed with white lawn chairs. The chairs were arranged as in a theater, two or three rows deep, and the people sitting in them stared straight ahead, as if at a movie screen. Though early in the morning, the elderly residents were already gathered. They waited and watched for sidewalk activity. They avoided turning their heads too often so that everyone seated could enjoy a type of privacy. Her small body bunched in among the others, Mrs. R. was able to relay her messages without creating interest or turning heads.

A little while after her whistle and comment about the sun, Mrs. R. felt someone take the seat behind her, a young man from the smell of him.

"Yes?" she said. "I'm listening."

The man behind her leaned down. "I entered the apartment not five minutes after your signal."

"And?"

"The apartment has no air conditioning."

"Incredible."

"I noticed a slight citrus stench."

"Go on," she said.

"I walked first to the couch, which greeted my entrance like a wide fat woman draped in paisley and defined by three cushions of flesh."

"Get to the point."

"Just one of the cushions is worn thin."

"Interesting."

"She sits only at a single spot."

"I'm way ahead of you."

"For a moment I sat there too."

"Gathering up your strength?"

"Believe me, I was tempted to go back to sleep."

"But you didn't," she said.

"No."

"You sat there half-awake."

"Yes."

"And lazily stabbed the cushions between your legs, hoping for a spurt of money."

"There was no point. It was cheap foam, well flattened. Nothing could be hidden inside."

"But you didn't check under the cushions?"

"No."

"Even for loose change?"

"I didn't think of it."

"And you call yourself a burglar?"

"I could stand to be more thorough."

"Go on."

"At arm's length from the couch was a television."

"How convenient."

"It allowed me to sit a minute longer."

"While you're resting, could I trouble you for a description?"

"It was a large TV, encased in a cabinet."

"Old?"

"Old? Yes, fairly, though a color set. On top was a doily and a candy dish. I let it be."

"Nothing you could carry out."

"No."

"And the candy? I would expect a stale mass melted together."

"No. Fresh. Replenished daily, from the looks of it. She likes her candy."

"It shows."

"Yes, she's a bit wide."

"A caribou."

"You exaggerate."

"You're not the one who saw her leaving this morning."

"No. I simply heard your signal."

Mrs. R. made a swathing motion across her breasts. "Like a strapless bra. That's all she was wearing on top."

"There must have been some looks."

"Her belly was soft as a mud pie, flung at the dirty eyes of the Al Lado del Mar, you can see the group from here."

"Yes, she's big, I admit it."

"Let's return."

"Against the wall of the living room was a large credenza supported on thin unsteady forelegs."

"Wait. What about the channel?"

"Please?"

"The channel. What channel was it on?"

"You mean the TV."

"What else?"

"I didn't notice."

"And you call yourself a professional, one of the best?"

"I'm sorry."

"Continue."

"We were at the credenza."

"Big and ungainly, you said. I heard."

"Yes. The credenza is stained to a dark walnut but I stroked it. It's not walnut."

"Do you mistake me for Ted Mack?"

"It's plywood."

"From her, who could expect more?"

"Of course I checked inside. The cabinet doors are even worse. Like styrofoam."

"You're telling me something new?"

"Bobbles right off the tracks. I could hardly open it."

"But you eventually mastered the styrofoam? A safecracker like you."

"Yes," he said.

"And once inside?"

"Not much of a booty. An album of ticket stubs and old telegrams."

"Did you read them?"

"I didn't have time. There was much more to do."

"Yes, I can see it. A mental giant like you losing his cool."

"Do you care to hear about the major centerpiece of the living room?"

"I can hardly wait."

"A round marble table. The marble was fake."

"That woman has a lot to answer for."

"It wasn't real marble, it was just painted to look like it."

"From the quarries of America."

"And covered thick with her life's regalia, trimmed in fool's gold."

"She should be assayed and cordoned off from the rest of society."

"At the front of the table, arranged like the flagship, was a servant's hand bell, white, with a gold-leafed handle like a papal cross. It was certainly not for ordinary use, perhaps something for the ceremoniously bedridden."

"Are you telling me what I can't figure for myself?"

"I'll skip the white ceramic bell from Holland."

"Please do."

"There was delftware as well as some Hummel figurines."

"You can skip it."

"It was an incomplete collection. I prefer cheaper ceramics. In school I used to press my clay through strainers to make long ornate strands. I was quite the talent . . ."

"You can skip that part too."

"There were photographs on the table."

"Let's hear it."

"First, an older man, in the heaviest gilded frame."

"That would be her husband."

"Yes. I checked."

"And why were you reading inscriptions, you the *Meisterdieb* so short of time?"

"I was checking the backs for hidden money."

"And was there any?"

"No. Nothing."

"Of course not. And you, a member of the elite."

"The photographs seemed to be arranged in order. Next was a picture of her son. Taken in Binghamton."

"Binghamton."

"That's in New York."

"I know where it is."

"He's an assistant bursar at a community college."

"She's got a college man? It doesn't seem possible."

"The other son is standing in front of the Museo del Prado. He's very small. The photographer tried to include the museum in the shot."

"A world traveler in her family? That I simply don't believe."

"It's in Spain."

"I know where it is."

"He's dead now. Killed overseas."

"Then perhaps it's true. What did the inscription say?"

"What I've just said. The Museo del Prado."

"Yes, where would you get a word like that? Do you know what city it's in?"

"Spain."

"What city? I'm asking."

"Prado. Prado, Spain."

She laughed briefly. "Don't let me interrupt, Mr. Sancho Panza."

"There was another photograph. A much younger man, a kid."

"That would be her grandson."

"With acne holes the size of tar pits."

"Yes, that's him. He's since had his face sanded."

"He must be the bursar's son."

"I can figure that."

"I left the photographs and headed for the bedroom, which I checked briefly and discreetly."

"Thou dost protest too much."

"Under the pillow was an envelope of cash."

"Did the envelope contain a letter?"

"No."

"No letter, even a slip of paper?"

"No, nothing."

"A handkerchief, Kleenex?"

"There was just money under the pillow, nothing else."

"And I suppose you took it."

Silence.

"I suppose you took it."

"Yes I did."

"And you have no letters or postcards to read to me?"

"There were a few scraps of writing in the album but I ran out of time."

"You the artist out of time? A crime to be rushed."

"All right, I admit I read them, but they didn't make sense."

"You mean you didn't understand them."

"All right. I didn't understand them."

"If you had taken the time to glue the pieces together."

"I'm sorry. The task was beyond me."

"And you call yourself an *homme d'esprit*."

"I regret it."

"You were too excited about the money. I suppose you ran tittering into her bathroom and explored her intimate bottles."

"Please. If I use the facilities, I stare straight ahead."

"I have the full picture in my mind."

"It's not what you think. I even brought you a gift."

"What do I want with this photo?"

"You can sell the frame."

"You sell it."

"I can't. They would be instantly suspicious. But you. No one would take you for . . ."

"A second-story artist?"

"Exactly. Especially if you bring your cane."

"I don't want it."

"I can't be seen with it, a young man like me with an antique."

"Take it from me. Throw it in the mailbox."

"She's here."

"Who? Oh dear, she's back. Take it from me."

"Her shoes. I meant to tell you about her shoes. Beautiful. Lined up neatly in her closet."

"With shoehorns?"

"How did you know?"

"A woman's intuition."

"Old shoehorns, too. Wooden."

"Not styrofoam or plywood?"

"Ha. I struggled to find you a pair but none were appropriate."

"High heels?"

"Terribly high, all of them. But they were dainty things, like glass slippers."

"On that piece of livestock?"

"Yes. Her feet are small as buttons. Take a look at her. She's getting out of the car."

"You're right. Her ankles are like icicles."

"Please, don't remind me of the heat," he said.

"How can she support herself on those tiny hooves?"

"It gives you an indication of her credenza."

"I can see. She's very unsteady, weight toppling her forward and a sandbag of derrière pulling her back."

"She's coming this way."

"Get going then."

He left without the photograph. She pressed it face down on her lap.

"Good morning," Carla said to her as she passed.

"Good morning," Mrs. R. said.

GRACE'S
REPLY

Grace's son joined the Navy at nineteen with vague but grandiose thoughts of espionage scuba diving. He drowned a year later. John's death was reported to her by men in uniform who knocked on the door. Their waists were tight and slim. It was a sailing accident, they told her; her son had been drinking. But Grace was sure he had been poisoned because he knew too much.

She remembered the day he left. She stood on the porch and cried. John pretended not to notice; he and his friend lifted their heads and yodeled some sort of war cry until Grace was forced to laugh. She held a finger under her eye to stem the tears. Then John shook his father's hand and as a last gesture of youth and frivolity jumped as high as he could over the door of his friend's convertible. He landed like a drunken sailor in the passenger seat. His leg had hit the door's partially opened window during his leap, but for Grace the flawed hurdle now resided in a memory that had perfected its arc.

Her son's sudden leap pierced her with feelings she had not seen coming. Her heart stopped as he drove away. It paralyzed her to remember it. Her nineteen-year-old son, struck down, would always be her nineteen-year-old son. He would always be jumping into a convertible like a TV detective. Forever young. Though a common enough theme, she embraced it like poetry.

She had always had this way about her. It was one of the things about Grace that set you wondering. She claimed to be an art lover, for example, but the only evidence of her taste was an oil portrait of herself. She liked to mention that the excellence of the painting lay in the fact that the oils would take decades to dry. It's worth it, she'd say, because of the vivid colors you get. To wit, the color of my eyes.

She managed to stand under this portrait of herself, with the frame-attached light aimed at the blue eyes, while a student from a community college interviewed her about her son's death. Grace had called the news stations about John, volunteered for radio shows, sent a telegram to Oprah. All for naught. Her husband steered her to the local cable station, but they told her they liked upbeat news for their community access hour. What about her other son? Maybe they could focus on him.

Finally a student from the community college came out to interview her for his final project. When Grace saw him, she couldn't help but gasp: he was so young, as young as John. He had brought his girlfriend with him. That was something John would have done, too. The student steadied his camcorder with one hand and held a microphone with the other. His girlfriend tried to move Grace away from the oil portrait to a neutral background. Grace refused to budge. She stiffened and became as motionless as the picture. Only her mouth moved, quivering slightly as she claimed that the autopsy which the Navy refused to perform would have revealed death from poisoning. Her eyes glazed to match the illuminated painted pair.

There was something obscene about two pairs of the same eyes staring into the camera. The student let the metaphor speak for itself. "Are you sure this isn't a pigment of your imagination?" he asked. He began stepping backward to bring more and more of Grace's living room into view. He panned the furniture and bookshelves. The books, selected for their height and binding, were like the slight mispronunciations of the self-taught.

And Grace was self-taught, if it came down to that. She was business path in high school, but it put her in too many typing

classes. She didn't want to type. She wanted to own something, run a business. Her boyfriend had a car that she confis-
cated; mornings she drove it to school with the best of intentions, dropped off her girlfriends, and then flowed on by the
school parking lot and onto the highway, her body drumming
to a beat, her posture perked for a change of plans. Eventually
she dropped out of high school, but she found herself missing those morning commutes gone astray. The peculiar air of
a school-year morning had taken her initial good intentions
and subsequent truancy and mixed them into an alchemy of
happiness that somehow faded once her days stretched freely
before her. She married and had her first child at nineteen.
At twenty-three she had her teeth capped for no good reason
except added whiteness and rectangularity.

She was a pretty woman and yet she had always seemed
older than she was. Her teased beehive in the high school
yearbook made her look thirty. Even in her twenties you
could sense middle age in her: she ordered albums advertised
on TV and purchased a stereo/TV console at Sears. She steered
unsteadily through youth like an old person on a bicycle.
Even from a distance something gave her away. She was out
of her element.

But now that she was thirty-nine, she had grown into her
age. She looked the best she had ever looked. The platinum-
colored hair she had worn for so many years no longer looked
out of place on her. She sprayed and brushed it into a sen-
suous silver comma, up and around the ear and back to her
chin. It was the perfect style to highlight her eyes—the hair
seemed to draw back in respect for these two blue suns with
their rays of tanned wrinkles—but until now it was hair that,
like tattoos on a man, imposed certain expectations.

Even in high school she had dated older men whose hair
was parted far to the side and cautiously sprayed in place.
Shortly after high school she married a man who was regional

manager of a large potato chip firm and who drove a company
car. He had gone to college. His name was Jack and he was
thirty-five. He was quiet and too grateful for her presence to
issue orders or counterdemands or otherwise bother her. They
had two sons. John, the older, dropped out of high school in
his senior year and joined the Navy a year later. The other
son, Gerald, went to college and worried about his grades.

When John was twelve, he left every day to hit tennis balls against the wall of a nearby school. Some days he
scraped a pebble against the bricks and drew a strike zone so
he could practice his pitches. Either way he was always at
the school throwing strikes or serving aces. Grace often went
up to watch. John was a pale, slightly freckle-faced boy with
black hair. He had Grace's startling light blue eyes, but unlike
Grace his black lashes made them look scored by heavy eye-
liner. Two vivid circles of red appeared on his cheeks when
he played. His body was scrawny and all-boy, but his face was
disconcerting. He seemed to be wearing makeup on his lips,
his cheeks, and his eyes.

One day Grace walked up to the school and saw an adult
hitting tennis balls against the wall. The man wasn't very
good: he held his backhand like a flyswatter. One ball sailed to
the roof, and he dug into his pocket for another. When he saw
Grace out of the corner of his eye, he kept to his forehand. He
backpedaled and backpedaled to maintain a forehand. Finally
he came to the end of the wall and caught the ball. He looked
up at Grace as if surprised to see her.

"Johnny's mom, right?" he asked. He looked to be in his late
forties. His stomach was huge but solid. It had muscled out a
round sweat stain on his T-shirt. "He's over on the other side
playing baseball."

Grace called John's name. She heard, like an echo, someone
yelling "What?"

The man pointed his tennis racquet across the street. "I live over there," he said. "I see him here every day." He bounced the racquet strings off his stomach. "Got inspired. Thought I'd give it a try. So far I've lost five pounds." He wiped his forehead. "Probably a couple more tonight." He pointed to an expensive car in the parking lot. "By the way, that's not my Rolls-Royce."

Grace laughed.

"Mine's in the shop." He waited for a reaction. "Somebody dinged my Flying Lady."

Grace laughed even harder. She had a husky laugh that the man liked.

He walked toward her and extended his hand. "Name's Slim, by the way."

Grace looked at his belly. It was as big as a medicine ball. "Hi," she said. She felt her hand go limp in his.

"You have a nice son," he said.

"I have two sons." She sat herself on the parking bumper and her hand slipped free.

"Busy lady. And their daddy?"

Grace hesitated. "On a business trip."

Slim nodded at this and raised his eyebrows. "Let me guess. Real estate."

"No."

"Insurance."

"No."

"Something to do with a bank."

"No." Grace got up from the parking bumper and brushed her backside.

"Is it animal or vegetable?"

"You don't give up, do you?"

"I see you laughing," Slim said. "Is it something that takes place indoors or outdoors?"

"Both."

"This sounds fascinating. What is it?"

"Potato chips," she said. "It's not as stupid as it sounds."

"Potato chips? Of course! It's not stupid at all! Rippled? Barbecue? Green onion? Lightly salted?" He had her now. Each word sent Grace rocking with laughter until she was back down on the bumper and holding her sides. "Honest, Officer, I didn't touch her," Slim was saying.

John showed up as they spoke. "We've got to go," Grace said. "Summer camp."

"Summer camp. Both of them?"

Grace gave an embarrassed smile and nodded. "Tomorrow."

"Summer camp." Slim considered this. "Summer camp, potato chips. Potato chips, summer camp. Tomorrow." His mouth moved in sucks and slices. He looked up. "Perhaps I should see you to your door."

On the way home he told them that his real name was Charlie. Charlie Pascal Samarov. But Grace continued to call him Slim.

Slim stayed for dinner. Then he left but came back in time for dessert. Afterwards he escorted everyone to his car and lifted up the trunk. Inside were Army-green duffel bags and backpacks. The boys were delighted to dump their suitcases. He gave Gerald a compass and John a small hunting knife with a leather sheath. Grace hesitated at the knife. Slim shrugged his shoulders and held out his hands. "So the kid murders his tentmates."

Grace leaned against the car to hide her amusement from the boys.

"Yeah, I'm gonna murder my tentmates!" John's body bounced with an impatience to get started.

"A clear case of self-defense," Slim said.

"Don't," Grace pleaded.

When the kids had gone to bed, she fixed some drinks. Slim told her about his job. He was a Navy recruiter. There were all kinds of problems you ran into, he told her. "You wouldn't believe some of the stuff the Navy pulls. Ho ho ho. You wanna buck the Navy? Uh-uh, don't try it."

"What would they do?"

"What would they do? What wouldn't they do?"

"Like what?"

"Like I am not at liberty to divulge what. Let's just say they stop at nothing. Nothing. They called me up about a year ago, right? and tell me I don't have enough—uh—colored boys. Not black ones, browns. Spanyolies. Like I'm gonna find some around here. I've got a friend in New Jersey, okay? New Jersey. Surprise surprise, turns out he's got the same problem. Only reverse."

Slim thought this was the funniest thing he'd ever heard of. So did Grace.

"So I offered to trade some of my good clean wholesome all-American white boys for—you know, and it all worked out. We fiddled some papers, we diddled our quotas . . ."

Grace wiped her eyes and sighed. "I don't know why you make me laugh. You've got the knack."

"But, boy, I'll tell you," he said, "we've got some crazies up there giving us orders. Okay? Okay. Now one admiral—this is a few months ago—decides that—uh—you know, the Female Recruits, as it were, have a low comely percentage. The WAVES are not making waves, if you know what I mean."

Grace happily agreed. Not making waves was not one of her problems.

"They're dogs."

"My stomach hurts," Grace said. "Please stop. I'm telling you to stop but I don't really mean it."

"Now you, if they saw you . . . but that's another story. What we are talking about here are dogs."

Grace blew her nose into a tissue. "Oh dear," she said.

"So you can guess what happens. Orders—*requests*, I guess

I should say, let's be official here—come down from the admiral that he'd certainly appreciate seeing a—uh—Different
Breed of Animal. I.e., get rid of the dogs. Get some bazoo-
kas. Get some weaponry. It gets so bad that they start offer-
ing bonuses for this." He began tapping his head with his
forefinger. "Bonuses. So Slim starts to get an idea. The light
bulb . . ." He gestured as if twisting bulb into socket. "Goes
on. All systems go. Slim's circuits . . ." He gave her a wink.
". . . are erect."

Grace punched Slim on the arm with a pert little jab.

"Okay? Okay. Let's think this over. There's a beauty school
right down the street. Obviously they need business, right?
It's just a bunch of students. So I work out a deal with them.
I invest in a better camera, you know, so I can get depth and
angles, and I do some pretty serious shopping at Goodwill.
Long slinky gowns. Girdles. So I take my new recruits down to
the beauty school. I get them all done up, hairstyle, makeup,
makeup three inches thick—this thick, thicker than lasagna
—red lips, false eyelashes. Then, if they're buxom . . ." He
cupped his chest to show what he meant. "I load 'em up. I
haul in the low-cut gown, which I have to slit down the back,
throw over a feather boa to hide their fat arms and stomachs,
and take a picture aimed right at their grenades, if you know
what I mean. If they're short and squat, I photograph them
from the floor up. They come out looking tall and lanky."

Grace nodded cheerfully. Being short and squat with fat
arms and no grenades was not one of her problems either.

Slim patted her on the back. "I tell you, I really had to pull
some tricks. Now you, I wouldn't have to pull any tricks with
you. I'd love to photograph you in one of those gowns."

"Just a minute," Grace said. "Pour yourself another drink."
She left the room. In a few minutes she reappeared in an
evening gown.

"Now that's what I mean!"

"But you don't have your camera."

Slim looked thoughtful. "Hey!" he said. "I guess I'll just have to come over here tomorrow!"

"When the kids are at camp."

"I guess so. I don't see any other way, do you?"

"Just a minute," Grace said.

She was gone for several minutes this time. Slim took his drink and lay down on the couch. He closed his eyes. He felt someone taking off his shoes. He opened his eyes and saw Grace in a negligee. It was blue like her eyes. "Do you want to come in the bedroom with me?" she asked.

Slim looked at her. "That's a direct question if I ever heard one," he said. He unbuttoned his belt, jerking the leather flap from its hook as though ramming in a carbine. He rubbed his stomach, dyspeptic and hard, a solitary yearning bicep. For a moment his hand glided lower than his stomach and he winked. "I'll tell you," he said. "This is just about the most comfortable couch in the world. Right now I must be the most comfortable person in the world." He gave her a salute. "I love this couch. I'm telling you, I love this couch. Where'd you get it, Goodwill?"

Grace retreated alone to her bedroom.

The couch was empty in the morning but Slim came over in the afternoon. Grace had already returned from the summer camp where she dropped off the kids. She took a picture of them in front of their cabin. In a week, when she picked them up, she would take their picture again in the same spot. She liked these before-and-after shots.

At the camp one of the women in charge of the counselors had looked at John and then at her. "He's got pretty blue eyes," she said. "Like his mother." Grace was seldom complimented by other women. Usually they were either taken aback or jealous. This was a momentous occasion. She was thrilled. She wanted to tell someone. When Slim showed up, she told him. "I'm happy," she said, "and I don't mind saying so."

"You should be, baby, because you know, that is the God's truth," he said. "You do have beautiful eyes. We've got to do something. We've got to do something special."

Slim had brought his Polaroid. He showed her how he posed his female recruits. He took a shot of Grace from the ground up, one from standing on a chair, one in the shadows—"This is when they're really ugly"—and a few close-ups of her face.

Grace looked at the pictures. All the angles made her look out of proportion. "I guess it really works," she said.

"Don't you think it's time we got a little racier?"

"Sure." Grace laughed.

"So do I, but dammit all, we're out of film."

She shrugged.

Slim chucked her under the chin. "Aw, poor kid's already missing her little boys. Come on, let's just hop in the car and get some more film."

The Quik-Mart they drove to sat beside St. Rita's church, which was holding its summer festival. Slim parked his car and went after a couple of hot dogs. He ate one hot dog while checking over the other one. He appeared more anxious about the second dog, which he jiggled absently in the direction of Grace's breasts and crotch. They both noticed this at the same time. "Knew I'd get you perked up sooner or later," Slim said. Then he ate the other hot dog.

Several local artists lined the church's parking lot and hung their pictures on the clothesline that cordoned off the lanes of art from the lanes of food from the lanes of games. Most of the artists specialized in charcoal portraits, sketched on the spot. Their samples were hung up behind them like T-shirts drying in the sun. Grace strolled over to look. Fat women had lost their double chins; men had recovered their hairlines.

One woman sat apart with oil portraits lined up behind her and a Polaroid camera tied to her leg. She caught them looking at her. "I make a preliminary sketch!" she yelled. She waved a pencil in the air to illustrate. She lifted up her leg. The camera dangled from a strap around her ankle and Grace saw white underwear under her flowery skirt. "Then I take some pictures. And then I go back to my studio. It's ready in a week!"

Grace and Slim edged closer.

"Take a good look," the woman continued. "This is an *oil* painting. This is not a charcoal fifteen-second caricature. This is art. Charcoal is okay for some. Watercolor, I'm not knocking watercolor, it suits many others fine. But oil takes years to completely dry. Years. There are not many things I'd be willing to spend years on, would you? To be honest—may I?— most of the faces I see I'd just as soon tell them: Forget it, it's not worth your time, you don't have the face for it."

"Look at this, Grace," Slim said. He pulled her over to one of the portraits that had a light attached to the top of the frame. "This is something. This is it, Grace. This is what I was talking about. With this thing shining down on your eyes."

"You have gorgeous eyes," the woman said. "I want to capture them. Beautiful and expressive."

"And with a light shining down on them . . ." Slim held out his palms. "Grace."

"You'd be an angel."

"Does the light come with it?"

"Everything. Frame, everything."

"Hey," Slim said. "How about knocking off five dollars since we brought our own pictures?" He showed her the pictures he had just taken of Grace.

"I can't use these," the woman said. "They're too dark and out of proportion. I need something taken in the natural sunlight."

Slim raised up his hands in surrender. "Far be it from me to stand in the way of great art. Sit down and pose, Grace."

Grace sat down. "I don't know . . ." she said.

"You have beautiful eyes," the woman said.

Grace smiled. "You're the second person who's told me that today. And I'm not kidding and I'm not bragging on myself— I'm just repeating what happened."

The woman flicked her wrists like a magician. "Voilà! There you have it! Do you need any better reason?"

Grace looked at the woman's hands. Tight rings garroted each finger, and metal bracelets dangled from her wrists. "Are those rings going to interfere with the brushwork?" she asked.

"These are only for show, my dear. I paint completely denuded of jewelry or other affectation."

"Denuded," Slim said. He let out a whistle.

"My son has the same eyes I do," Grace said.

"Again! There you have it. Immortality. Progenation of the race. Can you think of a better reason?"

Grace looked at her. Her eyes flickered toward the woman's hands.

"Can you think of a better reason?" the woman repeated.

Grace hesitated.

"There's only one answer, dear."

"No," Grace said.

"That's the answer."

"How about like this?" Grace asked. She struck a pose.

"No no no!" the woman shouted. "Wipe that smile off your face. This is art. I want you pensive."

It took a while, but Grace finally managed to look pensive.

When they returned from the festival, it was late and they still didn't have any film. "No problem," Slim said. "We'll just pick some up tomorrow. When does Big Daddy come home?"

Grace laughed. "Day after."

"Perfect. I just hope this doesn't get too serious because I'm starting to fall head over."

"Me too," Grace said. She sat down beside him on the couch.

"If you're so crazy about me, don't I even get a little drinkie?"

Grace jumped up. "Excuse my manners!" She ran to the kitchen and came back with two drinks and a photo album. "That's me," she said, pointing to some pictures of herself as a teenager. Her hair was teased a mile high.

"Jesus, Grace," Slim said, "you look like that little girl who married Elvis."

"That's me too," Grace said, pointing to another picture. She was older and there was a little boy by each knee.

"Your hair got a flat tire," he said.

"Here's another one." She directed him to a picture of her in a bikini.

"Damn! Don't do this to me, Grace. I'm burning up. I'm afraid to turn the next page."

"And that's my husband there."

"What's his name?"

"Jack."

"Jack's an old fella, ain't he? Gives me some hope. You must like 'em old."

"It's true, I do," Grace said. She moved her hand to Slim's stomach and began to massage it. It was hard and explosive. She wondered if it would start to sweat during sex. These were the kinds of thoughts she often expressed aloud to alarmed friends.

"You've got a cannonball waiting for me," she whispered in his ear.

"This ain't no cannonball," he said very loudly, as if to an audience. "This here's a bowling ball." He patted his stomach. "And this bowling ball wants you."

Grace began to sit on top of him.

"Why don't you slip into something more comfortable first," Slim said, holding her at bay. "And would you hunt me down some Di-Gel or something?" he called as she turned the corner.

When she returned, Slim had the television on. "Am I psychic or something, Grace? Answer me that one. Do you believe this? I say I'm a bowling ball and what's on the tube? A bowling tournament live from Canton, Ohio."

Grace was naked.

Slim turned up the volume.

"It's high," the announcer said. "The three-six pin. Thumb went down early on that one."

Grace moved over and stood next to the TV. Slim kept his eyes glued to the screen. He adjusted the contrast.

"You're throwing the ball sixty foot this many times," the TV announcer commented. "The fatigue factor has got to take over."

Grace paraded in front of the screen. Slim looked down for his drink. Finally she sat down next to him. "Here's your Di-Gel," she said. She left the room and came back with her clothes on. She threw him a pillow and sheet and walked back toward her bedroom.

"What, no lovey?"

"If you want!" She turned around.

"Oh Jesus, he missed the bucket!" Slim screamed. He jumped up and flung an imaginary bowling ball. "The Bucket Crumbler missed the bucket!" He sank back on the couch exhausted.

"Goodnight," Grace said.

She continued to see Slim every now and then, although that was the last night he stayed over. But every time she passed the incandescent eyes of her new oil portrait she thought of him.

During John's eighteenth year, Grace ran into Slim in the

grocery store and nothing was ever the same again. She looked down in disgust at the mountain of hamburger meat in his cart. "Boy Scout troop," he explained.

"Boy Scouts?" she said. "Well, speaking of Boy Scouts . . ." She cleared her throat. "Speaking of Boy Scouts, my little Cub is a Boy Scout no longer." She paused to admire her opening line. "Ever since you gave him that hunting knife and told him to murder his tentmates," she added for good measure. She went on to tell him that John had dropped out of high school. He was hanging out with the wrong kids. He was starting to get into trouble. "So what am I going to do about him?" she asked.

"A nice kid," he said. "Eyes like a girl. A good backhand. Not as good as mine . . ."

"This is no time for your jokes." Grace picked up a few pounds of his hamburger and flung it angrily into her cart.

"I need that meat, Grace." Slim's fingers inched cautiously into her cart.

"This isn't funny. This is my son. I would like a suggestion." Slim shrugged.

So Grace gave him her suggestion. Boot camp. John needed discipline. A makeover.

"Boot camp . . ." he said. "It's not a bad idea. Those were good times, Grace."

"Oh shut up," she said. "And just do me a favor. God knows you owe me one."

She pointed a finger so dramatically that Slim drew back in fear. He searched his mind for the debt he owed. "Anything," he promised.

"Convince John to join the Navy."

Now she could kill herself for saying it.

At times she would stop dead in her tracks. She saw John hurdling over the convertible. A cocky, immortal leap.

She should have listened to Slim's Navy stories—the things

the Navy did, the way they got rid of you if you knew too much. She should have listened.

She began to write letters. She persisted in the belief that John had died under suspicious circumstances. She wrote to the president, congressmen and senators, Billy Graham (ear to the president), Jack Anderson, the Pensacola Police Department, the Game and Fisheries Commission, Burt Reynolds (influential in Florida), *60 Minutes*, the American Civil Liberties Union, Bruce Berube (a friend John had mentioned in letters), and the Navy itself.

The Navy wrote to the senator who wrote to her. John had drowned while on unauthorized leave from the base. He had been drinking.

Of the others she wrote, only Bruce Berube, the Navy friend, replied:

Thank you for the check, it will come in handy. Maybe he was poisoned like you say, I can't say for sure. Because John knew a lot of things but he wasn't saying. He kept his cool. He kept his mouth shut and his fists open. Everyone loved him. He was just like a brother to me, he's got a girlfriend he was going to marry before he drowned. She's about to have a baby who's your grandson, she's got no money and she refuses to marry anyone else she loved John too much. She has a lot of pride but write to me if you can do anything for her.

Within a few weeks a regular correspondence had been arranged with Bruce as the liaison between Grace and John's pregnant girlfriend. "She don't speak English," Bruce explained in one of his letters.

"Neither does he," said Grace's husband Jack. He did not support her in this venture. He wanted to bury John. He had already suffered enough heartbreak. A stroke had left him with a useless left arm. He tucked it under his belt to keep it from straying.

"No English. That means her eyes are brown," Grace said. It was very important that the baby have John's blue eyes, which John in turn had inherited from her.

In the time spent before any photographs of her grandchild arrived, she read about heredity. She learned how to draw genetic tic-tac-toe charts to predict eye color. There was not much hope. The browns always outnumbered the blues. Only a 25 percent chance if the mother had a recessive gene for blue eyes. No chance otherwise. And if she didn't speak English, Grace thought, chances were she was brown through and through.

But she kept drawing her gene maps. Maybe the results would change and blue would come out ahead. She wrote to Bruce and asked him to find out the color of the mother's eyes. Bruce wrote back that the baby, a boy, had been born the week before. He had blue eyes and his name was John. Grace asked for a photograph. She enclosed a check to cover Pampers.

Her husband kept away from it. He consoled himself with thoughts of his other son, who had just made the dean's list in college. He stayed outside in the yard. Grace watched him hit fungoes with a plastic ball and bat. Forced to do everything with one arm, he had purchased something advertised on TV called a pop-up batting practice kit. It allowed you to throw up balls with your foot by stomping on a pneumatic tube. If you jammed your foot down hard, a fast ball came surging out of the tube. If you torqued your foot, a curve ball came out.

From the window Grace watched Jack try to master this machine. The plastic, corrugated pump that shot out these balls looked like a caterpillar spitting eggs. The balls came out crazy. With each swing his useless left arm flew out like a boomerang and bounced back against his side. She wondered if the neighbors were watching too. If she hadn't been grief-stricken she would have been embarrassed. Because he looked ridiculous. But he kept at it every day. Every day he asked Grace to shag the fungoes he hit, but she refused. Usually she didn't even answer him.

One afternoon he caught her watching him from the window. He came back upstairs and forced her out, practically pushed her outside into the spring air. "It's spring! Grace, it's spring!" he called. Grace shuffled lifelessly down the stairs, hoping to irritate him—*anyone*—with her dead weight, her dead grief, her sadness heavier than a body. Jack pulled her into the garage where he sat her on a bicycle. "Just do it for my sake," he said. "I've been practicing."

Grace sat on the bicycle like an Indian chief and remained mute. She watched vacantly as Jack attached his left hand to the handlebars with Velcro strips. "I've been practicing," he said. "Watch this." Then he pushed off, pedaled once with his right leg, and fell off. She sat there and listened to the sounds of his failure. She heard the rip of Velcro. He tried again. Fall. Velcro ripping. Velcro being reattached. A pedal clicking. Velcro ripping. She heard it all but she looked studiously in the opposite direction. It had been weeks and no photograph of the baby. When Jack got to the end of the driveway, he turned around. "This is great!" he yelled. "Come on!"

She pedaled reluctantly to the end of the driveway. Then she took a break. She decided to walk up the slight incline that took her to the stop sign. Without a word or sidelong glance of acknowledgment, she walked her bike past Jack, who was frantically pedaling once or twice, catching himself, and then pedaling again. He was not making much progress. At the stop sign she turned right. When she could no longer hear the crunch of Velcro, she stopped. She supposed she should wait for him.

Then she decided not to wait. Why should she? What had

he done for her lately? How many letters had he contributed?
She pedaled two more blocks until she came to the school
where John used to hit tennis balls. Across from the parking
lot of the school was the dead end where Slim lived. She rode
down the street and stopped in front of his house. The door
was open but she could see nothing through the screen. At
the bathroom window, whose frosted glass was pushed up,
Slim's face appeared behind the screen. His features widened
into a brief look of panic and then disappeared. She jumped
off her bike and ran toward the house. She slammed against
the door just as he arrived to push it shut.

She grunted and threw her hip into the door. "Let me in!"
she screamed. The door was shutting. She shoved her hand
into the crack that remained. "Okay, break my hand!" she
yelled. "Go ahead, break it!"

He opened the door. His face was red and steam rose from
his scalp and stomach. The towel that he held was too small
to go around him. He held it in front of him like a matador's
cape. "Just give me a minute," he said.

"I have a bone to pick with you, Mister."

Slim slowly backed up toward the bathroom.

"You didn't come to my son's funeral. You didn't send a
card. You got him into this mess and you didn't even send
a card."

Slim ran into the bathroom and slammed the door.

Grace pounded on the door. "Come out of there!"

Slim reappeared in his boxer shorts and T-shirt. "I'm sorry,"
he said. "I really am. I thought I sent a card. I remember
mailing it." He shrugged helplessly. "I'm sorry."

Grace was at a loss. She couldn't find the proper words. She
had no words. There were things seething inside her.

"What about that oil painting?" she finally said. "I thought
you were going to pay for the oil painting."

"Jesus, Grace, I forgot all about that. It's been years. Has it dried yet? I thought I told the lady to send me the bill. I remember mailing her something."

"You remember mailing just about everything, don't you? I'm the one who got the bill. What about those other things you told me? You know the Navy did something and you're not helping me find out."

"Honey, I never told you that."

"You're the one who told me what they did."

"Honey, now wait a minute, you've just got to calm down. What are you doing out here riding your bike in this hot weather?"

"I'm riding with Jack," she said.

"Where is he?"

"He's slow. For God's sake, Slim, the poor man's had a stroke! Don't you have any mercy!"

"Grace, now calm down, baby. I want to tell you something. Honey, I've been thinking about you. Grace, would you believe something?" Slim moved toward his monaural record player. It was turquoise with a white plastic turntable. "I've thought about you so often I bought this record. Reminds me of you, Grace. I want to play it for you." He leaned down and fiddled through his records. "Do you know Dan Fogelberg?"

"No I do not know Dan Fogelberg, not to change the subject or anything, Mr. Slim Slime. You think I'm not on to you?"

"You must have heard this. Listen to this. Grace baby, listen to this."

A guitar and voice began. She knew immediately that this would be a sad song. "*Met my old lover in the grocery store.*"

"Remind you of anyone?" Slim came up behind her and slipped his arms around her waist.

"*Snow was falling and . . .*"

"Well, not that part. This is really an all-seasons lullaby."

The song continued. The tinny voice of the singer matched the plaintiveness of the song. It was about a man who met

his old girlfriend by accident on Christmas Eve. They sat in
the man's car and drank a six-pack and talked. The woman
was married to an architect who kept her warm and safe and
dry; she would have liked to say she loved her safe architect
husband, but she didn't like to lie.

"*Said she married her an archi . . .*"

"A Potato Chip Man," Slim sang into her ear.

Grace smiled and leaned back. She sank into his body and
felt his stomach at the small of her back.

"Now here's your line coming up," Slim said. "Here it
comes."

"*I said her eyes were still as blue oo hoo.*"

"That's your line if I ever heard it," he whispered in her ear.
"That is your line."

Grace felt the breath in her ear. She turned around and
found Slim's earlobe. She moved her lips to his mouth and began kissing him. They were deep kisses that pushed him backward. Her kisses became more desperate. Slim's legs buckled
and Grace landed on the couch. He undressed her. His hand
attacked her breast like a rubber plunger; he sucked it hard
into his palm. He pulled off her pants and got down on his
knees to remove her shoes. He stood up with the shoes in
his hands. "Let me get these damn things out of the way,"
he said. He walked into the bedroom and rattled around. She
heard a theatrical commotion. There were muffled thumps
and bangs as he threw things in and out of his closet. "I know
I had a shoebox around here somewhere," he called to her in
a loud shout.

Grace lay on the sofa, studying the ceiling, the walls, listening to the excavation in the other room and his earnest
shouts of minor progress. Eventually she sat up and sighed.
She leaned down and snapped up her bra. She buttoned her
shirt and looked: her son's leap into the convertible sprang
into her mind's full view like the jump itself. The hurdle was

so perfect it stopped her breath. John could beat even the rules of gravity. Those who remained behind were all victims of gravitational pull. All but one. She would write to him someday. Congratulations on your blue ribbon, she'd say. I'm not surprised you won it in the high jump. Your father was quite a leaper too. One time he jumped over a whole car. I'll never forget it.

A
M I N O R
F A T A L I T Y

The heat wave in August was so severe it caused several deaths. Fredericka was among the stricken. She was a woman of great flesh and even without the heat she lived dangerously, her heart overlarge, overburdened, and overnourished.

While temperatures soared each day, a citywide dependency on air conditioners eventually caused brownouts. Fredericka and her husband used portable fans, and as these ground to temporary halts, her body temperature flew up and down like an elevator. During power shortages she retreated to cool bathing waters, but each excursion to the bathtub was all of a mountain-climbing expedition, requiring painstaking footholds, leverages, and extra bars hammered into the walls like pitons. By the time she was safely settled in the water, her body was on fire from the effort. In the bathtub she closed her eyes and dreamt of winter. On those distant snowy afternoons, hands tucked into her waist and the sun tucked into its shadow, she had often envisioned herself in the warm folds of a beautiful and much-lamented passing. But when her time came, she died instead a mere corpse, stark naked and cold as ice.

The heat continued for two more weeks, but Fredericka's husband was safe from its threat. He was not old enough, not infirm enough, and not heavy enough. Like these insufficiencies of age, illness, and fat which saved him from the temperature, his personality was also distinguished by an odd quality of not enough. It was both a good and bad thing: it had steered him through sixty-five years of living without meeting danger or creating an impression. In his job at a men's health club, for example, he had seen a few old-timers carted from the steam room with heart attacks. But he was safe from that. He had never used the steam room. He had handed clean towels to men the same age as he without ever thinking he should join them. In the same way, he had looked at families, their homes, their children, even the kinds of groceries they bought, without ever thinking any of it was meant for him.

His sister Filene told him to get on the ball. Now that Fredericka was gone, he could do things, she told him. Lots of things. Sell Herbalife or Amway or do some traveling. But he wasn't cheerful or bold. He could never fly to foreign lands. He could never be a salesman. His brave smile would tremble at the thought of knocking on a stranger's door. His sister, however, had just returned from two weeks in Japan. She could knock on anyone's door. But she was younger and had never been tied down. She was a spinster and yet she could mysteriously turn the tables on him. She called him "Forlorn Lorne" and laughed at him. On her return from Japan she had given him a foolish statuette of an old man and woman lifting up their kimonos.

She was with him at Fredericka's funeral, and people might have thought they were a couple. They sat alone in the front pew. He felt cut off from everyone. The family problems he kept hearing about on TV—teenagers and drugs, hyperactive and autistic children—only made him feel more left out. He wondered why he had denied Fredericka's drinking; it was a common problem now for everyone, movie stars and kids, and it could have been the one thing that connected him to the people he saw on the screen.

Looking back on it, he was sure that the drinking had con-

tributed to Fredericka's death. When the heat hit, it was as
if the defender cells in her body were too drunk to react.
Her blood pressure soared with the temperature and even her
fat maroon cheeks, like two heavy biscuits, felt the strain
of holding themselves up. She heaved herself into a cold tub
while Lorne unloaded a tray of ice cubes into the water.
Fredericka began to kick at the ice like a juggler kicking hats
to his head, but the cubes pooled at her toes, where they
were needed least, and the frantic useless exertion sealed
her doom.

Then, when a fine cobweb of purple leaked onto her skin,
Lorne panicked. He rushed to the Quik-Mart for a five-pound
bag of ice, but by the time he returned she was already dead.
Slumped on the toilet in defeat, he found himself merely an
observer: watching, staring uncontrollably and without emotion as air escaped her corpulence and bubbled in the bath-
water. It seemed to him that as her bodily functions had
dominated her life, so did they now punctuate her death.
The water bubbled again. He followed one of the bubbles as
it floated languidly before dissolving and his own thoughts
floated with it into nothing. He sat for a long time before his
sister prodded him toward the phone.

During the next few weeks, as he cleaned out Fredericka's
closets and found the hidden bottles of liquor, the image of
this bubbling water resurfaced again and again, reminding
him of tonic, of club soda, and of seltzer, and soon in his own
mind he had fashioned her as dying immersed in that same
beverage that had poisoned her. He found several bottles of
Old Grand-Dad hanging in the pockets of her shoe apron and
was thus able to gauge her decline as the liquor escalated in
proof from shoe pocket to shoe pocket.

In the shoes themselves, thrown into a colorful heap on
the closet floor, he found smaller bottles of every variety.
A couple of years before, having found in the toes of her

patent-leather pumps two miniatures of Tanqueray gin, he had, in another of his monosyllabic gestures, simply thrown the shoes away in an attempt to deal with the problem. Now, confronted with a multitude of shoes he had never seen before —bright jogging shoes that stretched enough to hold a flask, and rainboots that neatly tucked in a fifth—he realized that for every pair of shoes he had thrown away she had immediately bought two others, and that not only had the drinking problem grown worse, it had also cost him a great deal of money. He stared at the shoes, piled on top of each other in mounds. Grim reminders, bodies, green skeletons. There was some small comfort in this. He had paid in advance for her death; he could get on with his own life now.

This is exactly what his sister was telling him. She had been telling him this for years. She had never approved of Fredericka's obesity. She was ashamed of how it made Lorne appear, of what people were saying about a man who chose a woman who so thoroughly outsized him. Battered-wife syndrome—she kept hearing that on TV. But with Lorne, wife battering had been a physical impossibility. It was impossible to take over your knee a woman who could burst through the planks of a wall as easily as going through the door. It should at least be possible, theoretically speaking, for a man like John Wayne to take a woman like Maureen O'Hara over his knee, but whenever she imagined this scene with Lorne and Fredericka as the players, she was left only with a barren fantasy and the sound of splintering wood.

Though her brother and sister-in-law had hardly ventured beyond their hometown, Filene had seen Europe, Mexico, Canada, and parts of Africa and Asia. She went on Garden Club tours of New England, she rode the trail of the Wild West with the AARP, beheld the Great Wall of China with a Pacific Delight group, marched with the Blue Army to Fatima, and after each adventure, whether to Cheyenne or Nanking, emerged fresh as a daisy from the tour bus and surveyed her hometown depot with the keen eye of the magnanimous. She tugged crisply at the lapels of her jacket and turned to her disembarking bus friends, greeting each one with a smile and a nod.

Lorne and Fredericka would watch like hungry groundlings from their station wagon. They sat in the car and viewed the proceedings until Filene, without ever having appeared to notice them, positioned herself next to the mounds of luggage, inhaled deeply, and smoothed the hem of her jacket over midriff and backside. Eventually she swung her chin regally in the direction of the small parking lot. The station wagon bounced for joy. Wilted, rumpled—it never failed to be a hot summer day when she returned from somewhere—they ran to greet her. Perspiration ran into Fredericka's smile like tears of joy. Filene's face was cool and dry from the air conditioning. Caressing her neck were the fresh blossoms of a chiffon scarf. "My dear," she exclaimed softly to Fredericka. After each journey Filene was infected with a strange benevolence.

On the rides home Filene described her adventures. She used her vacation words:

Delectable.

Palatial.

Refreshing.

Most refreshing.

Her descriptions swayed with narrative buildup. She portrayed characters she had met or almost met or never met. There were no indirect quotations. Filene became the medium for her characters and rendered them directly.

"And then the *Bürgermeister* spoke."

"Only then did the toreador break his long silence."

"And thusly did the pharaoh speak!"

"And then our Nubian waiter bent close to me and said . . ."

Her speech surged forward with clauses modifying more

clauses so that the sentences ran on and on, yet remained oddly grammatical. As she narrated, her hands constantly fluttered with the scarf around her neck as though adjusting the volume in her throat, modulating tone, mixing sound. She was in fact cutting a demo for her speeches at Eastern Star. In the station wagon at least, she played to a rapt audience.

Lorne always enjoyed these times. He thought the three of them were great friends. He never sensed any tension, although he wasn't unaware of the fact that Fredericka and his sister were very different creatures. His sister, for example, was very careful of her furniture, which she protected with antimacassars. Fredericka, however, was apt to break furniture with her weight. This, over the years, had made her nonchalant and casual, an easy-come easy-go attitude toward chairs and such.

He remembered the visit from Fredericka's nieces and nephews, years ago. One of the boys cut himself playing outside and spilled blood upon the sidewalk. His sister made him scrub the walk before he came inside. Still, brown stains were left on the cement, and the electric stiffness of Filene's spine and hair let everyone know her displeasure. The nieces and nephews never came again, and he and Fredericka were asked to visit them only once, recently, at a wedding not long before the heat wave struck. Filene went with them despite the fact that she was leaving in two days for her trip to Japan. And although it was Fredericka's niece who was getting married, Filene somehow stole center stage by announcing a delay in her wedding present so that she could bring them back something from Japan. "Did you hear that!" everyone cried. "Something from China! The international newlyweds," they said. "Now all we need is something from Italy!"

A few weeks later, back from Japan, Filene mailed off a pair of man-and-wife teacups as her wedding gift. The heat wave had begun, but she appeared unaffected as she bustled about her kitchen and living room. She showed the cups to Lorne and Fredericka before wrapping them. Lorne was thinking, Man-and-wife teacups, what does that mean? He was expecting something like the cologne set he had once seen where the contours interlocked. The handles of the teacups must fit into each other, he thought. But when his sister showed them the cups, there were no handles at all. One cup was bigger than the other; otherwise they were exactly alike. The cups fit into a snug wooden box with Japanese calligraphy painted on the lid. The box seemed to exude a slight aroma of incense. As simple as the teacups were, they seemed exotic and different.

Filene lifted the larger cup. "This is the man teacup," she explained. "It's bigger. Because men often are." She let Fredericka hold the smaller cup. "And this is the wife," she told her. Her eyes swooped meaningfully from teacup to Fredericka and back.

Then Filene presented them with their gift, a ceramic figurine of an elderly Oriental couple. It was wrapped in layers of tissue paper. Filene caught Lorne looking over at the teacups as Fredericka unwound the tissue.

"Well, I couldn't get teacups for you two," Filene said. "They're not an accurate reflection of your sizes."

So he and Fredericka got the figurine of the elderly Oriental couple. Lorne could hardly look at it. He thought it was obscene. In the figurine the old man and woman were hiking up their dark kimonos to reveal enlarged and grotesque privates. They were assuming the posture, particular to their gender, for going to the bathroom. Lorne quickly rewrapped the figurine in the tissue paper.

Filene's face tightened with anger at his lack of gratitude. "I bought this at the foot of the Great Buddha in Kamakura," she said, "and these things are considered sacred in the Japanese culture." She ripped off the tissue paper and rolled it into an unusable ball.

But he found Filene's explanation hard to believe. Fredericka's struggle was obvious by then, and she had been incontinent at her niece's wedding. It was the first time he sensed there might be some animosity between Fredericka and his sister. Had Filene been spying on them at the wedding?

He realized of course that his wife would never fit in in a country like Japan. She would never fit period, Filene said. The doorways were smaller and the tables very low. People sat on the floor without their shoes. "It is not a *floor*," Filene told him, "it is a *mat*, and Fredericka would embarrass you completely by attempting to squat on it with her legs tucked under her knees. Her fingers are too fat to manipulate a chopstick," she added, "or, as we say over there, *ohashi*."

Filene, upon any return from an overseas trip, always went through this kind of cultural reentry period lasting longer than the actual journey. She was just becoming acclimated again when Fredericka died. Fortunately, she appeared at Fredericka's funeral in Western clothes. Lorne saw her touch a handkerchief to the corner of each eye. His sister was not one to cry openly. He assumed this was the result of being exposed to various forms of discretion in many different cultures.

Fredericka, however, cried easily—at fondnesses people on TV showed for each other, at beer commercials and the National Anthem, and at anything about very ill children having a wish come true. She followed radio talk shows hosted by psychologists and she took seriously their exclamations of concern and affection for their callers. In certain restaurants, not realizing a mirror was behind her, she beamed at all those who smiled her way and patted their hair. She had a good heart, Lorne thought.

On the same day that his sister explained to him about tatami mats and the diminutive size they required, he picked up Fredericka at the air-conditioned library and found her in

the children's section. The table in the children's section was
very low, like the ones they used in Japan. Fredericka was
sitting on one of the miniature chairs and looming over the
table like a mountain over the horizon. The librarians looked
sternly in her direction. He could tell from the size and color
of the book she was reading that it was for children. Because
of the heat, she was dressed in what amounted to a huge slip.
Her moist hair hung down in bangs and sideburns. When she
laughed softly to herself at something in the book, he felt a
sadness catch him off guard. He couldn't explain it. Usually
he liked it when she laughed.

They left the library and met Filene for dinner, and later
the three of them watched TV. When Fredericka cried during
one of the shows, she seemed to have trouble breathing. There
had been air-contamination warnings all day but, like tor-
nado watches, nobody paid too much attention to them. On
his way to the Quik-Mart for ice, he vowed to take seriously
all TV warnings in the future. But he was too late. His sister
knocked on the bathroom door as he sat slumped on the toilet. We would have called an ambulance, they seemed to say
to each other. We would have. But we never thought.

Who could have predicted?

The afternoon faded into dark without his ever
getting up from the chair to turn on the light. On the TV
he heard a mother talking about her schizophrenic son. She
showed some of her son's artwork and began to point out
clues. She turned the pictures upside down and sideways. Em-
bedded in the dark heavy textures, like spiders in a forest,
were scratches and black wiggles. "These are the clues," the
mother said. Clues to what? he wanted to know. He didn't
understand.

Most of the shows concerned themselves with marriage in
one form or another. So far none of the forms matched the

form his own marriage had taken. If what the TV had to tell him was correct, he was one of those people who should have never married in the first place. He almost hadn't. And Filene almost had. Another second here, a forward or back step there . . . Things would have been much different.

"That's enough," Filene said. She walked into the room and turned off the TV. "My friends want to know what's wrong with you."

"Can't they understand?"

"For heaven's sake. That was months ago!"

"I still think about it. Even when I'm watching something like this . . ." His arm raised limply toward the blank screen. "It reminds me. It has nothing to do with . . . I can't get it out of my mind."

"You've got to get out," Filene said.

"Maybe I should get my job back at the health club."

"If it comes to that, I guess so. My friends want to know why you're behaving this way. Lorne? What am I supposed to tell them?"

He shook his head. Filene's friends had charged to the rescue, introducing him to several widows. It seemed there were widows all over the place. He had no idea men usually died off so quickly. Now Filene was insisting upon introducing him to someone else at the public meeting of the Trustees of the Library. She said this woman was very special. Not like the other one, she promised. He had spent an evening in the apartment of a woman introduced to him, and she had sat at a TV tray and written thank-you notes while he watched the TV channel devoted to a closed-circuit surveillance of her apartment lobby. He got to meet several more women, at least from a distance, as they went in and out the lobby door. A couple of days later he received a thank-you card in the mail.

He didn't want any more of that. He could see what Filene and her friends thought of him by the type of women selected for these introductions. Even his sister misunderstood him. He would have to move to an entirely new city if people were going to look at him in a different light. There had been too many embarrassments with Fredericka. He looked over at the figurine of the old man and woman lifting up their kimonos and remembered the wedding of their niece. He hadn't hiked up his kimono, but what he'd done was almost as bad. The whole world had seen it. During the ceremony, embarrassed and worried about Fredericka's recent incontinence, he had hovered about her and ignored the other guests. Then, at the reception in their niece's home, Fredericka sat for a long time on a couch. He nervously fetched her drinks and watched her disregard them. Her eyes had dropped to a point above her knees and she appeared to lose interest. Even the lure of food, laid out before their eyes on the buffet, failed to stir her. He tried to prod her. When she was resistant, it was like moving a filing cabinet. There were no good handholds on her. He grabbed a portion of her arm and pulled. Enough of her lap moved to reveal a wet stain on the couch. People were moving toward the table of food. "Nobody will notice," he said. "I'll sit on it and you go get cleaned up." As her bottom inched up, his own inched down. He sat on it all afternoon. He felt like a hen. But he was willing to do it for Fredericka's sake.

For the rest of the afternoon he watched her. She had already forgotten him she was so caught up in the celebration. She followed each tray of hors d'oeuvres and champagne, she smiled as she watched others smiling in their groups, her eyes watered at each heartfelt greeting to the bride. Her face, and the flat smooth shine her features had become, reflected the joy around her. But as the early summer pumped bellows of heat and happiness onto the wedding celebration, Lorne was left with a sadder feeling of time running out.

If only I had done something, he thought, I could have prevented it.

Filene placed a glass of wine in his hands. "This will make you feel better," she said. She turned on the news and sat back on the couch. During commercials she talked about the wonderful people who made up the library committee. "They're dying to meet you," she said. "You can't disappoint them. Lorne? Where are you?"

"Just get me another glass of wine," he said. His heart pounded at the kind of response he had given her, but without a word she stood up and obediently walked into the kitchen. She apparently thought nothing of it, but he felt a great sense of victory. He turned back to the TV. He was no longer an observer. The newsmakers were his comrades. He understood their problems. He had problems too. It was part of life. It was part of being actively engaged. On the news an old man from Italy took all his savings and traveled to the United States. The man spoke no English, but he had cousins in Oakland, California, near San Francisco.

Lorne smiled sympathetically. He had to laugh. Oh sure. *Everybody's* got a cousin in California. It's the same old story. But the old Italian man somehow wound up in a small town in Maine, population 229, that was also named Oakland. He looked and looked for his cousins. The town was smaller than they had described, but cousins in America were prone to exaggerations. Visit us, there's money on trees, etc. He asked people, as best he could, where Oakland was. Here, they said and pointed to the ground. Here. Carducci, he said. No Italians, they said: You got to go to Portland for that. Oakland! he repeated in frustration. Here! they said. You're here, man. What more do you want? Oakland, he kept repeating. Oakland. He hummed the Tony Bennett song. "I left my heart . . ." Finally they understood. "Oh! San Francisco!" they screamed.

The story circulated quickly, and all the townspeople in Oakland, Maine, gave a party in the town hall in his honor. They taped up banners that read SAN FRANCISCO. The China-

town booth served instant ramen and egg rolls, the Fisher-
men's Wharf booth served Maine crab and lobster, and the
Italian booth served spaghetti. No one could communicate in
a common language; there was lots of hugging and tears of
joy. The media grouped all the townspeople together with the
old Italian man at the head. He demonstrated the few words
of English he had learned during that week. "I left my heart
in Oakland, Maine!" he sang in his strong Italian voice, and
all the townspeople raised their arms and cheered.

Lorne was watching, hiding a tear, and thinking: I want to
go to San Francisco too—I would like for someone to take me
there. Even Peter Jennings had a smile on his face when he
said goodnight. Fredericka would be mopping her nose with
a handkerchief. In the middle of the night he would wake to
the sounds of her muffled sobs. I'm thinking about that man,
she'd say. That Mr. Arrivederci . . .

Don't cry, he'd plead. Oh little Freddie, please don't work
yourself up. Inside her a furnace was being stoked higher and
higher. Her heart was reaching its breaking point. If it hadn't
been the heat, it would have been Mr. Carducci.

He quickly lifted the glass of wine to his face to cover the
tears. Then he drank another; then another. His sister gave
more details of the library meeting as her own wine intake
increased. "You're going," she said. When he woke in the
morning, the words tolled like a bell. "You're going . . . you're
going . . ." What a headache he had.

In the fog of the previous evening he remembered the time
of seven o'clock, but nothing else. He assumed the Trustees of the Library would meet in the logical place. A little
before seven he stepped into the library and followed the
sound of voices to the basement. He checked for his sister,
but she hadn't arrived yet. He wondered why they hadn't
come together. Because he was being set up, he remembered.
With a woman. He looked around at all the women. They

were lined up at the coffee machine. There were too many old women, and all the old women smoked. They poured sugar in their coffee, grabbed a donut, and lit a cigarette.

He took a place at the end of the coffee line. One by one the old women turned around to look at him. It was as if they were a line of aging chorus girls, with high arching glances instead of kicks. Which one was he being set up with? he wondered. His face grew hot and began to itch. When he touched his mouth, he realized he was still wearing his ski mask. It was a wool balaclava pulled down over his entire face. He looked like a burglar. The flirtatious looks the women had been sending him were looks of fear.

He ripped off the wool balaclava, grabbed a cup of coffee, and scurried out into the hallway. His hands were shaking. Coffee splashed over the top of the cup. Such a fool!

Tonight it had been so cold he had searched the closet for his warmest wool cap. When he pulled the balaclava off the shelf, a miniature of Old Grand-Dad whiskey had fallen out of the mouth socket. Instead of throwing it away, he had tucked the tiny bottle into his front pocket. Now he took it out and poured the whiskey into his cup of coffee. He sipped on it for warmth. It was freezing out in the hallway. Libraries were built like crypts. He could feel the cold stone seeping through the soles of his shoes. It was hard to believe the weather had once been so lethally hot.

He took another gulp of the spiked coffee. Maybe Fredericka didn't have a drinking problem after all. Maybe he just wished she had. Maybe it was his sister who had the problem. Filene, when she was visiting and needed a drink, used to rummage through the bottles hidden in Fredericka's shoes until she found the brand she wanted. In return she brought Fredericka liquor miniatures from all over the world: adorable midgets of Sambuca, Suntory, Boodles. Less important than the names were the cute sizes and shapes: long-necked or hip-heavy runts, baby gourds and jugs, others with skinny widths like flasks. Fredericka's favorite was a peewee of Anis Machaquito with red tassles hanging from the neck and a picture of a matador on the label. She never hid this one in a shoe but kept it right on her dresser.

He walked back into the room. They were starting to take their seats. There was a lot of laughter. He tried to smile and look relaxed. People carried their coffee and cigarettes to their chairs. They continued smoking and drinking during the introduction. A short stocky woman took the podium, smiled, looked around, and settled her smile on him. Is this the woman? he wondered. He turned around in his chair, searching for Filene's ocean wave in the sea of hairstyles.

"Welcome," the woman said, "to the Tuesday night meeting of Alcoholics Anonymous."

Before he lowered his head, his body jerked with a guilty twitch.

"I see some new faces here tonight," the short stocky woman continued. He stared into the black water of his coffee. They could smell it on him, couldn't they? He covered the cup with his hand to trap the whiskey odor. "Don't be nervous," she said. "We're all your friends here." He glanced up to see if everyone was watching him. The fear that someone would tap him on his shoulder and point to the door kept him from following the first part of the meeting. He knew vaguely that business points were mentioned. Some milestones recognized. Gradually his trembling lessened as he realized nothing was expected of him. No one was going to hurt him or kick him out. He could just sit there.

In an unplanned yet orderly way, members of the audience walked up to the podium and said a little something. All of them began their talk the same way. They stated their first name, adding as if it were their last name, "and I'm an alcoholic." The audience answered back: "Hello, first name," they responded in unison. It had a certain rhythm.

My name is first name and I'm an alcoholic.

Hello, first name.

He was starting to get the hang of it.

My name is first name and I'm an alcoholic.

Hello, first name.

You could bounce your head to it.

My name is Lorne and I'm an alcoholic.

Hello, Lorne.

Could he ever be so brave?

My name is Lorne and I'm an alcoholic. A funny thing happened to me on the way to the Board of Trustees library meeting. Everyone would laugh.

Hello, Lorne, they responded.

Hello, he said back to them. I'm glad to be here. Hello.

F I N A L

W E E K S

Fifteen years ago I was a student from a Quaker college in Indiana who was abroad in Japan. I spent an academic year in Tokyo, after which I lingered most of the summer in the mountains near Kanazawa where I worked in a lodge. I grew close to the lady who ran this mostly deserted hostel, and when I left she cried. We promised to write, and at the more unlikely promise to meet again we simply nodded politely. I snapped my final pictures like last desperate waves from a car window and left.

The photographs I took during that summer were gathered in a growing bandolier of cartridges. Once back to Tokyo I hurried to the camera store where, stopping to collect the rolls from my handbag, I fumbled and dropped them all on the sidewalk. The film sprang loose from the cartridges and coiled at my feet. My first impulse was to throw my body over the negatives and protect them from the sunlight. But it was already too late. Passersby, sensing my shock, stopped in midstride. They gathered around me and looked down quietly at the black coils. Someone came up and patted me on the shoulder. I opened my handbag around my face as though it were a feed bag, and pretended to peer inside until I gained control.

This explains the gap in an otherwise unbroken line of pictorial autobiography. I have pictures of everything in my life, every person important or unimportant, chronicles of daily events, attempts at adventure, scenery shots taped together for broader mountain sweeps. They're all labeled and mounted chronologically in photo albums. You may think it's silly, but friends love it. They thus avoid slide shows with somebody else on the controls, and detailed narratives that don't know when to stop. Just look at the pictures, read the labels, get through it fast, and close the book. They love it. They never ask for more. They never hint for less. It's just right.

As the albums piled up over the months and years, the past became no more and no less than these pictures. Pictures missing were emotions forgotten. It became harder and harder to summon them up with photographic recall.

Now, for the first time in a long time, I've thought of those nonexistent snapshots. Instead of photographs, a letter is all I have. The ink of the letter is fourteen years old; black *kanji* crawl out of it like tired crustaceans. It's from Toda, the lady who ran the lodge. When I look at it now, I have the feeling of something barely rescued, a memory caught in the webbing of a glove before it flies out of sight. I used to be able to read it. It all used to make sense to me.

Toda ended her letter with the *kanji* for "sailing away" and calligraphed it to match its meaning. The tail of the *kanji* stretched across the paper until the ink drifted off the page and the letter ended as if on air.

I was finishing my senior year at Earlham when I received it. Earlham, a small Quaker college in Richmond, had a program in Japanese studies and a tatami room in its library that featured doors of *shoji*. Students liked to wet their fingers and touch the paper *shoji* until a hole appeared. Such was the extent of vandalism on campus.

The same dated tranquility could be seen in the town of Richmond itself. Its downtown swirled around a train station still in use. It was here that I liked to spend much of my free time. The Amtrak from Chicago stopped there; going home on this train during vacations, I felt thrown into a black-

and-white film from a previous era. There was something seductively obsolete about riding a train.

I remembered that train to Chicago when I left Tokyo and headed for my summer job on Hakusan Mountain. I was glad to be rid of the overcrowded Tokyo subways. For months I had ridden them in either total blankness or total hostility. Either way I had very unproductive commutes. Standing beside me in whatever contortion, my Japanese neighbors peacefully read their magazines. I never spoke to them except to murmur Sorry, sorry, sorry again, sorry. Tumbling against them, I was conscious of the lack of odors.

So I stepped into the old passenger train en route to Kanazawa with the feeling of relief. This was what I remembered. I was home again. Thoughts returned to me like breezes; I felt suddenly like writing a letter.

After the train arrived in Kanazawa, I rode the bus upward toward Mt. Hakusan until, two hours into the climb, the paved road ended suddenly like a nougat bar torn in half. There, in the small village that sprouted at the end of the bus line, I stayed overnight with a nasty-tempered old lady who made me wash her stairs. Judging from the bucket in her hand, she had been expecting me. The next morning I left with a crew of construction workers who drove me farther up dirt roads until we came to the point from which I would have to walk. The clutch burned as the truck plunged up wide, stripped paths. We pitched against each other, and the men looked at me and then nodded to each other. They yelled, "America?" I screamed, "Yes!"

After the truck stopped in a circular expanse, the workmen poured me tea from a thermos and then headed toward the sleeping necks of their backhoes. One of the men who had been sitting in the cab came over to the truck bed, wrestled out two poles, slung them over his shoulder, and said, "Let's go!" I put down my tea. When he saw that my cup was still full, he gestured for me to pick it up and continue drinking. I picked it up and sipped. He made a motion to chug it, but the tea was steaming hot. I sipped, he gestured to chug. Trying to do the right thing without burning my mouth, I spilled the tea and burned my chest instead. I ballooned out my shirt front with thumb and forefinger and shook it. Humiliation and pain forced a smile to my face. The workman never recognized my distress, which was good, because I didn't want to cause a scene in a foreign country.

I put down the tea and we climbed out of the volcanic mouth of construction toward the steep forest paths. A couple of hours later I finally arrived at the lodge where I was supposed to work. Outside, an old man squatted in the sun. His bottom did not touch the ground, but he appeared quite comfortable. A much younger man and woman stepped out of the lodge. The woman greeted me with a shy smile and a hesitant step forward like a British servant being briefly introduced. Beside her was a man whose horrendous buckteeth instantly reminded me of Jerry Lewis. This was her husband. I thought it was a joke. Sex? These two? Are you kidding? It was at times like these I wished for an American friend beside me.

The husband made grunts in my direction. "She can't understand that," I heard his wife say. His head bobbed vacantly in all directions until his glance settled on the ground. "Ah, she's your business," he said and threw out his hand in a ball-less pitch.

Yes okay, my mind retorted, but you don't know what I'm thinking about you. "I'm looking for Toda-san," I said.

Everyone stepped forward.

"Ha ha ha ho ho ho," the old man laughed. In a laborious series of movements, he had gone from squatting like a squirrel to resting on all-fours like a dog to slowly rising up like a bear. I liked the old man just from the effort he put into getting off the ground. I found out later he was the husband of the nasty old woman I had stayed with.

The younger woman smiled at me. This was the Toda I meant. She asked me quietly if I wanted to see the place.

I said yes. Neither of us moved.

Finally the old man waved his arm. "Go ahead!" he said happily. "Go ahead! Go ahead!" He was gaunt and hollow-cheeked and very cute. "That's right! You too! Go ahead! Have a good time, enjoy yourselves!"

We walked into a big room with a dirt floor and long tables. Toda cleared her throat. "This room is for the guests to eat in," she said. "There are no guests today. So that's nice." We moved quietly toward the kitchen, which was hidden from general view. In the corner was a picnic table where the family ate.

Opposite the kitchen was a tiny four-mat tatami room with a window. In front was a counter where people registered and paid. We wandered briefly toward the counter before gravitating back to the tatami room.

"It's nice," I said nervously.

Down the hall were segregated toilets with their huge country holes in the ground. Toda laughed with embarrassment. "They don't have these in Tokyo," she said.

"Oh yes they do. Don't worry."

She looked at me doubtfully.

"I'm used to it," I said.

"I'm sorry," she said. Then we fell silent again.

We walked back to the main room where a half staircase, half ladder affair led to the loft. This was where I and any of the tentless guests would sleep. The loft was primitive, but there was a clean improvised tatami area for sleeping. Except for here and the other tatami room, all the floors were dirt. Toda pointed this out. "It's very convenient. You can keep your shoes on."

"Yes," I said.

A couple of sleeping bags curled on the tatami like caterpillars. Toda caught me looking at them. Throughout the tour she had been sneaking glances at me. "Two other college students work here," she said.

I couldn't imagine why. There didn't seem to be anything to do.

"Ashida and Naoka."

I nodded.

"They're not women," Toda said. "They're men," she explained. "But I don't think . . ."

"That's fine," I said. I was used to neutral cohabitation with men. In one of my college's Quakerlike impenetrabilities, it had made the dormitories coed. Even the bathrooms. Outside the showers you had to turn a sign to indicate your gender; the opposite sex was requested (with that quiet firmness of a spinster teacher looking over your shoulder) to respect this. Sometimes you left the bathroom stall to see a boy washing his hands at the sink. Sexually ignorant, we coexisted on another rankly intimate realm. Perhaps the point was to take the sex out by putting the bodily functions in. It was hard to fall in love with the boy in the stall next door.

Toda said, "American girls . . ." Pause, nod. ". . . a lot, don't they?"

"My college doesn't allow it," I said.

She smiled. "Oh. I wondered. I hear things on TV."

"I see what you mean."

Toda nodded. She had a strange, calm shyness. "It's nice to be young."

"You're young too."

"Twenty-eight," she said.

"Oh. Well!" I mockingly exclaimed in English.

She cocked her head at me. I knew that I would like her.

We went back downstairs for some tea. The kitchen was damp because of its cement walls, and I was cold. I realized I had made a mistake in expecting summertime temperatures. Altitude. I hadn't factored that in. But I had never climbed a mountain before and had pretty much vowed on the way up never to do it again.

Toda left the kitchen while the tea steeped, and came back with what looked like a narrow cigarette case. "This will keep you warm," she said. A tiny stick of charcoal about the size of a cigarette smouldered inside. She wrapped the case in a scarf and tied it around my waist. The unit branded the small of my back. Instantly I felt heat. I saw Toda fight back a smile. "It's for old women," she explained. "This one belongs to my mother-in-law. You stayed in her house last night." She searched my face for a reaction but I didn't say anything.

She poured the tea and I looked across the table at her. The name Toda, given its auditory sibling in English, had been perfect for the old woman, whose toadish warts trimmed the neckline of her kimono. But this Toda was pretty. Country living had left her softly disheveled. Missing from her was the look you saw in so many Tokyo women, of being pulled tight, hair pulled tight and yanking the eyes into slits, mouth withdrawn and bitten on. The vinyl sheen of relentlessly black hair.

Toda's face was more relaxed. Her eyes were rounder, as if their corners weren't tugged at by the severity of hairstyle. Her own hair was a simple bushy pageboy, a charcoal-colored disarray that dipped low on her forehead in a slight widow's peak. She had a habit of turning her head so her fingertips, without moving, could skim across her forehead and into her hairline, sweeping any stray wisps along with them. There was something comforting about the slow-motion oddness of this gesture. Over the course of the next few weeks I often caught myself imitating it.

She asked me where I was from. "Chicago," I said. The old man walked into the kitchen.

"Chicago," she repeated. "Chicago. I've heard of that.

It's . . ." She smiled and shrugged. Now that she had begun the sentence she would have to complete it. "It's near New York, I think."

"The Great Lakes," the old man said. "You know that word!" He leaned close to my face. He was all skull and swollen cheekbones. "Great Lakes, ha ha."

"Yes," I said, quickly coaxed into being the proud student. "The Great Lakes."

Toda's husband walked in. "Tea," he said.

The old man prodded his son's arm. "Hooo. She understands everything. It's wonderful."

His son didn't answer. He could hardly close his mouth all the way, his lips couldn't cover the teeth. Did I hate him for this, simply because of the way he looked, his sorry buckteeth? Yes, I did.

"Would you care for tea?" Toda asked her father-in-law.

The old man bowed militantly and barked, "Thank you thank you very much!" He poked me on the arm until I watched him; then he repeated his bow. "Japanese tradition."

Toda's husband finished his tea and burped. Then he got up and left without having grunted another word to any of us. Toda sighed and refilled our teacups. The old man looked at his tea but didn't touch it. "More Japanese words!" he exclaimed. "More Japanese tradition! Osake!" He slapped me on the arm. He was hard not to like. His head looked just like a newborn chick's.

Toda noticed me shaking. She put the flask of sake in a small pot of hot water to heat it.

"This will warm you up!" the old man said. "It's not summer up here. We only have three seasons. I'm very lucky. I get winter twice a year and my age makes three. Ha ha. Do you understand?"

"Yes."

"It's so splendid," he babbled.

The small cups held only a few thimblefuls of sake. I thought if I gulped the first they would leave me alone for seconds. I was not used to drinking because it was not allowed at my school and I was an obedient student.

Strong rice wine, heated, an inability to hold liquor—soon I was hanging over Toda's shoulder and being dragged up the stairs. At my feet I saw the old man's hands. He was climbing up behind me on all fours. My loyal friend. They laid me out on a futon. The burn on my chest began to throb. Comforted by images of my own distress, I began to dream. A story unfolded that made perfect sense until I opened my eyes. Two guys were looking down at me. I smelled the aroma of briskly chilled skin.

"A foreigner," one of them said. He was a tall shadow with hair in a puff.

"It's time to eat," the other one said. He was a shorter shadow with stringy hair. He leaned down to me. "Do you understand?"

"Uh-huh," I said in English.

They burst into laughter. "Uh-huh," they repeated.

I sat up before realizing my shirt was open. At some point in my dream I had taken the trouble to rummage through my knapsack and unfold a wash-n-wipe against my burn. Now the cloth was stiff with an unpleasant lemon smell. Beside me were other wipes, thrown like used Kleenexes. Wow, I thought, I don't remember this at all. Alcohol.

"Do you have a cold?" the shorter one asked.

"No," I said. They continued to look at me as I tried to button my shirt with one hand and hold the wash-n-wipe with the other.

"Colds can be very dangerous."

"You have to take medicine very early to stop it."

"I don't have a cold," I said. "I burned myself."

The shorter one widened his eyes and pointed to his chest.

"Yes," I agreed.

"Oooh," they said meditatively. The two guys, whom I presumed to be Ashida and Naoka, turned to each other and discussed how this could have happened. The shorter one lit a cigarette, held it out to me, and said, "Like this?" He jabbed at my chest.

"Un-un," I said in English.

"Un-un!" they laughed. "Un-un!" They went back to talking between themselves. The burn most likely occurred, they agreed, when I splashed myself as I tested the water of the public bath in Kanazawa. "That bath is really hot," one of them said. "Did you go to the public bath in Kanazawa?" they asked me almost as an afterthought.

"No," I said.

They looked at each other. Not cigarettes, not bath water. They went downstairs to get Toda.

Toda arrived in a restrained state of panic. She was carrying a baby and a flashlight. Two other children darted ahead and then rushed back behind her legs when they saw me. She shone the flashlight on my chest. Ashida and Naoka looked over her shoulders.

Tiny blisters like Braille dots covered my breastbone. I pulled down my bra and saw that it had protected me. The burn ended in a V-shaped red cleavage.

"That's bad," they said to Toda.

"A burn like that can be serious."

Toda turned her flashlight to the stairway. A downy head appeared and then the tips of hands. The rest of the old man slowly emerged and crawled over to have a look.

"Trouble," he said. He pointed to my chest and drew a V in the air for the others. "Such a perfect shape," he said.

"Brassiere," Toda said. The old man and the two guys were down on the floor with laughter. Toda smiled.

Downstairs she gave me a thin towel to wet and keep

against my chest while she hunted for ointments. All she found was Chinese medicinal tea and harsh antiseptics for cuts. The old man claimed that he would go down the mountain in the morning and find some salve for burns. I protested, saying the burn wasn't that bad, which it wasn't. But Toda said she would be responsible if it got infected.

The old man hooted and poked me appreciatively. When he stopped laughing he leaned down against his knees and breathed hard. I didn't see how he could possibly make it down the mountain. The poor old guy climbed a flight of stairs like a man reeling from gunshot wounds.

When I saw him leave in the morning, his head sinking below the steep trail, I never expected to see him again. I saw him as one of these creatures in a myth, the blind man with a walking stick who throws magic stones into the lake whenever he needs to see. He would need such a miracle. Then I realized the miracle had already taken place: somehow he must have climbed up the mountain in the first place.

The best thing about my summer job was that I didn't have to do much work. People who climb mountains are the same kind of people who sleep in tents and cook their own food over campfires. All I did was write down their names (to much applause), collect money, and send them on their way to the campsites up the hill where Naoka and Ashida cleared sites of rocks and stumps and tried to establish some sort of plumbing, meaning deeper and deeper holes. Once in a while someone would run down from the campsite and pay me a hundred yen for a cup of coffee. Toda showed me how to make it: one teaspoon instant, one teaspoon powdered cream, two cubes sugar. Then I'd go back into the tatami room and rest until someone else came running down with a hundred yen. Word got out. Everybody really liked my coffee.

Sometimes these campers would try to engage me in con-

versation. They'd ask me things like did I like Japan, and I'd
say yes. They'd ask me if I liked Japanese food and I'd say yes.
They'd ask me if I knew what the prime minister's name was
and I'd say Tanaka. Then they'd ask if I liked Japanese men
and I'd say yes, what the heck, after all I was a representative
of my country.

Naoka and Ashida never asked me any of these questions,
but once at night when they thought I was asleep they had
a very long discussion about whether I was a virgin. Finally
they concluded they should just ask me, so they crawled out
of their sleeping bags and came over and began shaking me.

"Yes!" I shouted. "Now let me get some sleep."

"Why?" they asked. "Do you have to get up early and make
instant coffee?" They started sniggering.

Well, I liked those two a lot because they tried their hard-
est to be mean to me but it just wasn't in their nature. I could
see why Toda's two older children had grown inordinately
fond of them, dogging them everywhere as they went about
their chores. The youngest child, Hiromi, eighteen months,
stayed with Toda and me. She played quietly between us as
we conversed in the tatami room. Since there were no chairs,
we conversed lying on the crook of our arms. Inevitably, one
or both of us would fall asleep. Sometimes I would wake up
with a pair of eyes in my face and Hiromi perched over me
like a cat.

For Toda and me, the pace of life slowed to a drowsy sway.
We more or less hung out, all morning, all afternoon. We
drank tea and ate *senbei* snacks. Sometimes I made us coffee, my by-now-famous American, specifically Chicago coffee
(it's the *heaping* teaspoon that makes it Chicago, I explained
to a bemused Toda), and it seemed always these times that
we would look up from our cups to find her husband standing in the doorway. He was watching us in his vacant idiotic
way, mouth not fully closed through no fault of his own, but

I didn't like it. It made me sick. At some point it dawned on me that what I had been taking for crumbs of mud on his face was simply his unshaven chin. Now I couldn't look at him at all. But it hardly mattered. He didn't require a greeting of any sort, nor did he give one. He looked around, though there was nothing to see in the cramped four-mat room, and left. Again I wished for that American friend to whom I could turn for a mutual reaction. I realized suddenly that this was their bedroom as well.

"Doesn't he want me in here?" I asked Toda one day after he had departed.

"No, it's all right," she said.

"I'm sorry."

"No." Toda got up, pushed down into her slippers and fitted Hiromi into hers. "I have diapers to wash," she said. I followed her down to the stream. She did the cleaning part and I rinsed. A certain intimacy had been won, I felt, so I finally broached the subject of taking a bath.

"Every week or so," she said.

"Every week?"

"Or so."

"When's the next one?"

"I don't really know."

I said, "When will you know?"

"I don't really know."

"But you do have an *ofuro*?"

"It's in the shack." She looked at me and laughed. "That's why we don't prepare it very often. It takes time. Nobody's here all the time except me." She stopped. "I tend to forget about it. Do you want to take a bath?"

"Yes."

"I forgot all about it. Oh," she said. She wrung out a diaper with the most languid squeeze I have ever seen; just as slowly she hooked it over her forearm. "I'll wait until my husband leaves. You don't want to go in after him." She looked down at the diapers she was lining up along her arm. "He comes and goes," she said. In no hurry to finish, she seemed instead bent on using as much time as possible. "Because I know you don't like him," she said quietly.

"No. I like him very much."

"I don't like him," she said.

"I don't either," I said.

"I don't like him, a lot." She whispered it to me like a nun breaking silence, and turned bright red before my eyes. "Don't laugh," she said.

"I'm not laughing."

"Do you know this word?" she asked. She said a word.

"No," I said.

"It means the mother-in-law problem. It's a famous expression." She looked at me. "Because it's true." She picked up a stick and drew some *kanji* in the dirt. "See?" She drew them more slowly. I recognized the *kanji* for "bride."

"Oh yes," I said.

I drew a circle around the word. "And you've got this," I said.

"Everyone does. Especially in the country. You met her. You stayed overnight with her." She laughed. "Alone."

"She's a witch," I said. "Unbelievable. I couldn't believe it."

"What did she do?"

"She didn't say hello, she didn't give me tea, she didn't ask me what America was like. She gave me a bucket of water and a washrag and told me to wash the stairs."

"That's her. That's what she's like. She does it to me too."

"She didn't let me watch TV."

"That's terrible."

"It's like . . ." I stopped.

"What?"

I snapped my fingers. "Cinderella," I said in English. "A movie, a fairy tale. Never mind."

She said a word in Japanese that I didn't know. "You mean that?"

"Yes, I guess so. Why don't you get away from her?"

"In the summer I do. Up here. My husband's usually down there too. It's better. Even though I'm all alone."

"You have your children. And Hiromi is the cutest baby in the world."

She smiled. We started back toward the lodge. I found my-self devising easy plans of escape for her—get a divorce, tell off your mother-in-law, go to Tokyo, meet someone nice. It was all very American of me.

"Well, you know," she continued after a minute, "in the winter we don't take so many baths because we don't get dirty. It's like winter up here. So you don't get dirty."

"I'm dirty," I said.

"It's the same in Tokyo," she said. "Did your Tokyo family take baths in the winter?"

"Yes," I said.

"How often?" she asked.

"Every day. Or every other day."

"Every day? A very progressive family," she said thought-fully. She walked ahead of me, then caught herself. She turned and waited.

The next morning her husband left with the workman who had led me up Mt. Hakusan and who reappeared every few days with more poles on his shoulder. Eventually, Toda told me, they would have telephones on the mountain. "Then you can call me in Tokyo," I said.

As soon as her husband was gone Toda walked to the shack that housed the *ofuro* and began preparing the bath. It was the old kind, heated by a fire underneath. Toda explained it to me. I waved her off. "I know all about it," I said when she told me to be careful. I waved to her from the doorway with a washbasin pressed against my stomach.

The shack was unheated and cold. I washed quickly on a

pallet whose wood had grown slimy and then lowered my shivering body into the tub. I had to squat high in the tub to protect my burn from the hot water. By now the burn had dried and splintered into a perfect cleavage of cracked red clay. Though it no longer throbbed, the skin had shrunk. If I straightened my shoulders suddenly, some of the cracks would widen and ooze.

I crouched on my tiptoes and balanced myself on the wooden slats that kept me from direct contact with the red-hot bottom of the tub. The slats were removable and thus movable. They rode several inches high to prevent scalding by the hottest dregs of water, but nonetheless I could feel the heat growing too extreme at my feet. Because of my burn I wasn't balanced well enough to swirl the water effectively. I stood carefully to get out. As I swung my left leg onto the slimy pallet, the heel of my right foot pushed through the slats and touched the searing iron bottom. I lurched into the air as though by electric shock, fell on the pallet—snapping its wood into the shape of my butt—and skated into the wall. Another burn, a good one that sizzled, more panic among my keepers. Still it was worth it. I was clean, I was warm from the inside out. For the first time in days I felt totally relaxed. I lay on the pallet until I dried like a dish on the rack.

The burn on my heel forced me into even less usefulness. Knowing it wasn't serious, I was in no hurry to get well. I walked along with an inept, limping shuffle—left foot scraping, right foot on tiptoe. Part of it was due to the burn, the other to the condition of my shoes. The spines of both my tennis shoes had long been broken from my habit of wearing them like slippers. But it didn't matter. I could hop easily from the tatami room to the counter to register any campers.

One day, like something up from the fog, there he was— the old man was back. A couple of arriving hikers told us an old man was a little ways down the trail. Toda and I walked to the edge of the clearing and saw him worming himself over a fallen log. Once on the log he just lay there and rested. We went back inside the lodge and sat at the kitchen table until he came in. "Oh my!" Toda said in surprise when he finally crept in. "Oh my, oh my." She stood up in welcome. The old man leaned on his knees, head down, and flicked his hand in acknowledgment. Still not looking at us, he produced the ointment. Then he sank sidesaddle onto the bench and rested his body against the table.

I went into the bathroom to apply the medicine his rescue mission had produced; the ointment was especially welcomed on my chest for I had been hunching my shoulders as the burn contracted. My heel was still in the inflamed stage. Its blisters felt thick and topographical and, like a Band-Aid, not attached to me except at the edges. I suddenly realized life up here left me an awful lot of time to think about these two spots on my body. I had begun to mark their progress like a pregnancy, hoping to produce something more at their termination, something that lived beyond the daily grind. It was almost frightening what I'd sunk to. I was plunging my stakes into two tiny burns, wishing they were a little bit worse. What if these two little burns were two little kids? What in the world, I wondered, could Toda's life be like day after day?

When I awakened from my thoughts, I was looking down at the huge country hole that formed a toilet. In the swamp of excrement below floated one of my tennis shoes. I hopped into the kitchen. "Come here," I whispered to Toda. I pointed to my shoeless foot.

Toda got a mop and followed me into the bathroom. I directed her to the hole and there was my shoe still afloat. The level of the waste was high enough that the mop handle could reach it. When it was this high, you could check on all the activities of the guests. You could see their problems, their time of the month, all the things you knew about but didn't want to be reminded of. It was very gross.

"This is extremely embarrassing," I said.

Toda shrugged.

"These are the only shoes I have or I wouldn't make you do this."

"It's nothing," Toda said. "It goes on all the time."

"I'm so humiliated."

"Don't be," Toda said casually. "I jumped in one of these once. My son fell through when he was six. He was in the hospital for three weeks."

"Don't tell me anymore," I said.

She stopped.

"Then what?" I asked.

"I jumped in after him," she said. "It was over his head but not mine."

"You fit?"

"I had a hard time getting out," she said.

"Oh stop," I said.

She jimmied the handle.

"Then what?" I said.

"The worst part was the old woman. The old woman wouldn't let me in the house."

"Wait a minute," I said. "I thought this happened up here."

"It did," Toda explained. "We had to take him down the mountain to get him to a hospital. She wouldn't let me in the house."

I nodded.

"I was dirty," she explained.

"I see. Listen," I said, "why don't you just leave her? And him. Why don't you leave?"

She shrugged.

"You can come to Tokyo with me."

She pulled back the handle. For a moment the shoe dangled. "Almost," she said.

"Well?" I asked.

"I can't," she said. "Everyone will know by my accent that I'm not from Tokyo."

"That's a good reason," I said.

She laughed. She bent down to get a better look at the shoe. "These country toilets are very dangerous for children."

"That's all you're going to say?" I asked. I bent down and saw that she was smiling.

When she stood up, my shoe was hooked neatly on the end of the mop. We brought it up and looked at it. Strangely, neither one of us was particularly repulsed by the sight. She looked up from the shoe. "You must have a lot of boyfriends," she said.

"I don't think so."

"How many?" she asked. "Five?"

"Four," I said.

"Four." She mulled this over.

"I was kidding," I said.

"Oh. But you've had a boyfriend, haven't you? I mean, you've been kissed, haven't you?"

"Well, yes, I mean, God of course!"

"What it's like?" she asked.

In my mind I repeated "God of course!" hoping it hadn't sounded the way I had originally meant it to sound, like "Everybody's been kissed!" My mind recoiled at what came next. "Everybody but you, that is." It was too painful even to consider. I dismissed the thought at once.

"I've never been kissed," she said.

"Oh," I said. "Oh no."

"People say it's really nice."

"I feel really bad," I said. "I didn't mean to . . . if you want, you can kiss me."

"Thank you. I appreciate it. You're a good friend."

"I feel bad," I said.

"It's romantic, isn't it?"

"No. It's not."

She laughed. "You are funny," she said.

"Besides, you've . . . you know, you've done . . . you know. I don't know the word," I said. Which was a lie, because it was about the first word I learned.

"Three children," she said.

"Well, that's proof. So that's even better." I looked at her, so calm, so nice, so pretty, shit all around us, all these things ahead in my future; and the electric hidden empathy I felt with her I remember, but I also remember it was just a college phase. When I left the mountain I couldn't look at her face. I hid behind my camera and shot pictures instead. I disappeared down the trail, keeping my eyes glued to my feet. I searched for stepworks of roots. Suddenly I could have been anywhere.

"I'm sailing away," she wrote me fourteen years ago, the words themselves made to drift into inklessness, into my own absorption. But today when I hold the letter in my hand and open it again, the characters that once leaped to my senses now gather in a lifeless blur. I can no longer read a word it says.

T H E

M E T A L

S H R E D D E R S

When I describe my job, I put on a bit of an act. I'm not completely honest about it. But dishonesty works, I've discovered, especially at these get-togethers where everyone shows up with a six-pack. Guys throw out a "So what do you do?" feeler as they sit down with hands tight around a beer bottle. Bored, nervous, with accusatory glances toward the spouse who made them come, they nod lifelessly at the responses.

This is where I enter the scene. I start talking about my managerial position at the Metal Shredders. Within minutes, the white knuckles are gone; the hands start to relax. Pretty soon they're leaning back enjoying it. The wife is off the hook.

"You're kidding!" they say after I relate a few job anecdotes. They're laughing. I'm apt to laugh myself. Somehow it doesn't seem so bad from the safe distance of a Saturday night. But the fact is I hate my job. Every morning I bury my head under the pillow until my wife drags me out. I'd rather die than go to work. But I'd rather go to work than tell my father I quit. "I'm quitting John Bonner & Son Metal Shredders, Dad. I'm not working for you anymore. I'm leaving you. Yes, Dad, I'm betraying you." I'd rather die than say it. In fact, I'd rather go to work. Every morning it's the same vicious circle.

But at parties I weave a few tales, all of them true enough, though you tend to embellish after a few beers. If I find the details getting out of control, I look over at my wife, staring at me with that stoic disgust she saves for when I'm naked (gaining weight recently), and it reins me back in somewhat. Besides, with this job even the truth is serviceable. And it's certainly true from my point of view that my employees form the crudest, most malformed group of men on earth— half Dirty Dozen and half Three Stooges. Yet these men I claim to despise are the very swine that string the pearls of my anecdotes. Even the dead employees liven things up. Listeners' eyes grow wide with half-drunk amusement. First I get them with the story of the human shredding. Then I follow it up with the wild dogs. After that, anything I say is funny. But people who are drinking have no taste. Though they may appear to be sloppily attentive, their minds are actually a blank.

The truth is that my job is excruciatingly dull. During the course of the day I have the time and appetite to eat about four brown bags of lunch. On occasion the workers have thrown their lunch pails into the small refrigerator near my desk, and I have been driven to furtive acts of theft, greedily opening their treasure chests and wolfing down tidbits that wouldn't be missed. I haven't reached thirty, yet I'm growing fat. Being a redhead, that means pudgy thighs and a stomach that's excessively white. At night I suffer pains after supper. My wife thinks it's an ulcer from working so hard, but it's just from eating everything in sight and washing it down with cups and cups of burnt coffee. Because if it's one thing men can't do when they're left on their own, it's make a decent cup of coffee or keep their toilets clean. When you face the kind of toilet I do every day, what's a rancid cup of coffee to that?

Besides, I don't work hard enough to warrant an ulcer. I sit at my desk. I sit at my desk. Am I repeating myself? I do, every day. Sometimes I stare out the window at the metal waste surrounding me. Other times I take both fists, slam them to the desk top, and exhort myself with a cleansing

"Okay, let's do it!" Then I throw myself into work. Once in a while my wife calls; having twisted herself into a knot, she's unraveling fast. It's not just my ulcer she's frantic about. She's convinced my ulcer is responsible for her lack of pregnancy. I don't have an ulcer, yet I feel telling her this might not be entirely welcomed news.

At any rate I sit here at the Metal Shredders, wishing instead I was scurrying about to important meetings in some I. M. Pei office building, running down marbled hallways, silk tie flying, briefcase swinging, slapping the elevator door as it closes in my face. Not the wildest fantasy perhaps, but it's better than the yellow and pink carbons that have stained my hands the color of a lifelong smoker's.

Right now I'm going over Accounts Receivable. The books are a mess. I'm not keeping up my end. The debits don't equal the credits, not that they ever have, and now I have to send out the bills again. Bonner Senior says I don't need a secretary, but I do. Someone to address envelopes. Put stamps on them. Find a mailbox. Make a decent cup of coffee and throw a PowerBoy into the toilet. I can't stand it. I'm planning to go nights for an MBA. An MBA should rocket me out of here. With offers storming in even my dad, Bonner Senior, won't want to hold me back.

I look out the window. It's depressing here. The office is a prefab aluminum box with a flat roof that frightens me during snowfalls. In the summer I worry about frying like an egg. Even with a fan turned on my face, my insides boil so bad I might pop. I could go outside, but that means having something specific to do. The office is built on stilts, and I would look pretty stupid walking down the steps and standing at the bottom doing nothing until I was so embarrassed I simply walked back up. I know this because I've done it. So I'm stuck up here. Thus, the four brown bags for lunch.

Presumably I'm up here on stilts so I can see what's going

on. This means I have a panoramic view of stacks and stacks of wrecked cars. I feel like a demented air-traffic controller madly conducting crashes. And what is going on under my watchful eye? My workers hide out during the day and emerge at night when it's time to go home. Working, sleeping, or drinking, I don't know. When they want to hide, even binoculars can't find them. During lunch I might see them playing Mad Max with Uzi water pistols. They're very much into these kinds of games. Man against scrap metal. One feeds the other, it's a symbiotic relationship between workplace and futuristic metal movies.

The Shredders, with its high rises of scrap as the buildings and the greasy apron as our future farmland, displays a nuclear winter already in progress—bizarre metal appendages, fossils of Skylarks and Chryslers from the twentieth century. Man-eating machines. It's the new classic confrontation. It's true that one time a machine really did eat someone; we had an accident and he slipped right through the tunnel of the shredder with barely time to scream. The shredder is fast and powerful. It hardly does to say it wasn't a pretty sight. It was hardly a sight at all. But that's another story. A story, I'm sad to say, I tell to friends whose usual reaction is to laugh their heads off.

And during the rest of the day when the workers aren't playing Mad Max? If I see them at all, they're under the hoods of their own cars, then under the hoods of their co-workers' cars. To a man they drive horrible bombs, disgusting big hunks pieced together with junk from the even more disgusting cars we've shredded, and after barely making it to work only to break down at the entrance, they spend all day fixing them so they can barely make it home. The paycheck never makes a round trip either. Overseeing them is not what I envisioned as a career. That is, a Business Career. You think:

People who take taxis

People who know what checkbooks are
You don't think:
Squished cars
Men who squish cars
Stealing their lunches
Being within a hundred miles of them

I go back to Accounts Receivable and try to bear down. But my eyes keep wandering to Accounts Payable and all these invoices that don't sound familiar. There's a bunch from Laskow's U-Pullem. Who's been pulling what? I'll have to ask Bonner Senior about this. He often does things without telling me.

It's quiet now at my desk. Outside, the noise is stopping. The machines are powering down. The shriek of metal slows to a high scratch; I shiver until it's over. There's no traffic beyond the fences. Suddenly it's very quiet and it's like one of those things, a hammer bashing you over the head. It feels so good when it stops. The silence is wonderful. I lean back and listen to it. It feels good. I put my feet up on the desk. I'm in charge of the place. Just great. And I close my eyes.

The door is kicked open. Tony, our arc welder, walks into the office and strides over to the time cards as if he owns the place. He picks up the cards and shuffles through them. I barely, just barely, open my eyes and glare at him. A thick fur runs up his forearms, onto his upper arms and into the sleeves where it burrows under his T-shirt in a buoyant layer. Even through the hair I can see the speckles of welding burns on his skin.

Tony stands by the time clock. "Hello Tony," I say in a monotone. There's no answer. I think longingly of my MBA.

From the deck of time sheets Tony selects a card. He looks at his watch and makes an obvious gesture of checking it against the clock. "Mr. Greenjeans is late again," he says.

This time I don't answer.

"More than his usual half hour."

"Those seats have to be welded in," I tell him.

"I got some nice cream-colored upholstery," he says.

"Well slap it in. Do some welding for a change."

"Jesus it stinks. You'll never get that smell out. I can't even go near it."

We picked up a car declared unsalvageable by the county attorney because of the odor (some corpses stored in the trunk). My dad has a friend, Mike Charny, who works at the county attorney's, and we get a lot of interesting junk coming our way from their office. This one is a good deal. An '86 LTD. Mechanically it's perfect, but the interior has been ruined. We're going to throw in some new seats and a bunch of air fresheners and put it in our auction.

"Well go near it anyway," I tell him.

"Go near it anyway, he says." Tony picks up the beaker from the Bunn machine and swirls the coffee. "You got a cup? And I tell you another thing," he says, grabbing the mug from my hand and thrusting it in my face. "Them dawgs going to come around. That's dead meat they're smelling."

"Well clean it up for Crissakes."

"Listen to him. What'd I just tell you? I put a bandana around my mouth. I still can't go near there. It looks like Greenjeans to the rescue."

"Leave him alone, Tony. He's just our night watchman. He's an old man."

"The smelling section of his brain is gone."

"How do you know?" I ask. This kind of interests me.

"He had an operation knocked it out."

"What operation when?"

"Brain surgery. I don't know!"

My legs are still plopped up on the desk. Tony walks over to me and looks down at my crotch. "I need in," he says. He drives his hand between my legs—I barely avoid clocking him on the jaw with my boot as I jerk down my legs—and fiddles inside the drawer of my desk.

"Don't get nervous," he says.

"What are you doing, Tony?"

"I need the key to the tow truck."

I fling his hand aside and dip my fingers into the well that holds the tow truck keys. They're gone. "What do you need them for?"

"Your old man has a job for me."

I lift the tray and search the rest of my desk drawer. "Where the hell are they, Tony?"

"Anybody sign out?"

We start scattering papers for the clipboard that's not hanging on the nail where it should be. Tony finds it by the coffee machine. The last entry is not only coffee-stained, it's over six months old. Tony shrugs, brushes and straightens the top page like it's a wrinkled shirt, and hangs it back on the nail. Coffee-yellowed, it seems as ancient and discarded as the concept of organization behind it. Tony reads the page. "Supposedly Thompson was the last person to use it."

"That helps," I say. I lean back and laugh. Thompson is dead.

Tony grabs a chair, swivels it around, and hikes a leg over it. "You've got a great sense of humor," he mumbles. Then he plops his chin on the backrest while he stares into space with the rubbery-faced intensity of a bulldog. Thompson was a friend of his—not a great friend, but a friend. He and Tony succeeded in transforming the Metal Shredders into a brewery and personal car repair shop. Too much of the first and not enough of the second led to his demise.

For years there's been talk of a pack of wild dogs in the area, and Thompson proved it wasn't just myth. He broke down not too far from here after going with Tony to one of those desolate bars that always manage to spring up in desolate places. Thompson knew about the dogs of course. They were legend, often talked about but never quite seen directly except by the friend of a friend. A lot of people didn't buy their existence at all, but Thompson must have believed it enough not to start walking but not enough to stay locked in his car. He stood out on the hardtop and worked under the hood, and I suppose being drunk destroyed his reflexes or his hearing. It scared us all when we found out, but there was a certain thrill to it too. Frankly, it was the first time I was glad the office was built on stilts. If Tony knew the story I told about it, prefaced by a hilarious description of his friend (extremely short with arms as long as an orangutan's), I don't know what he would do to me. Well, now I can add a punch line to the story: at least Thompson did one thing right before he died. He signed out the tow truck.

"Tony," I say, "it suddenly occurs to me that you used the tow truck the day before yesterday."

"I put the keys back," Tony mumbles. Now he's staring at the floor and his mouth is open and sucking the back of his hand.

I hold up the invoice from Laskow's U-Pullem. "So is this you?"

Tony raises his head long enough to give me this look, this look that says, How stupid can you be? Then his face, smooth from stretching toward me, plops back on his hand and is instantly mushed into oatmeal.

I reach down to my bottom drawer, try to open it, kick it, remember to crack the top drawer to unhinge it, and reach down for the rest of my food. I'm reluctant to bring it out because I'll have to offer some to Tony and I want it all for myself. But I have to have something. I've got to eat.

I bring out half of a turkey and cheese submarine from Lawson's and pick off the cellophane. (My lunch is augmented in pit stops at several stores during my morning commute—I'm even embarrassed to tell my wife how much I'm eating and too embarrassed to buy it all in one place.) The guts of the sub have gotten nice and soggy, the way I like it, and I grab a bite before reluctantly holding it out to Tony, who shakes his head no. Just as I'm inwardly celebrating his refusal he asks, "What else you got in there?" I make an elaborate show of looking down in my drawer to find him something good. My hand brushes aside a Drake's apple pie and I resurface with a rock-hard, skinny cigar of jerky. "Slim Jim?" I ask.

"Un-uh," Tony says. "I'm in the mood for something sweet. You got anything sweet?"

At first I'm convinced that Tony, having heard the telltale crinkle of cellophane when my hand hit the Drake's pie, is just being a sadist. When I toss him the pastry, he rips off the wrapping without even bothering to check what fruit flavor he's received (unless he has package colors memorized, green for apple), breaks the crescent pie in half, and devours it in a continuous gulp with three spasms of his throat that pass as bites. To my complete surprise he hands the other half back to me, having some notion of fairness after all, and appears to give the pie no further thought. I don't think he even noticed what he was eating, and just as briefly as he savored the taste, he now seems to have forgotten completely about it. This is like sex, I think. This is how a man is supposed to be. This is how I'm not. Ask my wife, no don't.

My wife. Thinking about her does me no good. I squirm in my seat and my face grows hot. Tony's face is still mashed into the back of his chair. It's about time to go home. But I have a few minutes. I reach into my drawer and pull out my Slim Jim. When I hear rattling on the metal stairway, I chomp quickly and throw it back into its hiding place.

The slow-climbing footsteps have a crisp hollowness that reminds me of autumn. Tony is about to say something smart about the footspeed of our night watchman when the window reveals the bold gray hair of my father. Tony jumps up as soon as he notices him. His lower body is an empty pyramid where he's standing over his chair, his upper body a masquerade of attentiveness.

My father opens the door and does a stomping routine as though it's winter out (it's late spring). "Been welded to that chair since yesterday," he says.

I watch as Tony goes from at-ease to attention. He swings his leg over the backrest and brings his thighs together. He fusses with the chair, rolling it on its casters until he has it arranged under a table. But he makes no response. After all, Bonner Senior could have been addressing me.

My father takes off his jacket with excruciating precision. We wait silently. Then he turns and fixes a neutral gaze on Tony. All I feel is relief.

"What?" Tony finally says, shrugging. He quickly twists up his palms. Bonner Senior doesn't answer and Tony gets nervous. Having nowhere to go, he walks in a circle. With all his hair he looks like a caged animal.

Bonner Senior doesn't bother with any niceties. He just says, "Why were you sitting down?"

"Well, Mr. Bonner . . ."

"Do I pay you to sit down?"

"I was trying to discuss the time card situation with Mr. Bonner. I mean . . . not you, I mean your son."

It takes a lot to make Tony call me Mr. Bonner. Watching him squirm isn't pleasant. I know how he feels. My stomach starts to burn. I feel a flush creep up my chest.

Bonner Senior straddles the corner of my desk and aims his crotch directly at Tony. "I guess this means the car's all done?"

"I have located the problem," Tony says. This is his answer to a yes-or-no question.

"And?" Bonner Senior throws out his hand like a friendly politician fielding questions.

Tony responds by looking at me. His glance is followed by my father's.

"The car's outside," I say.

"And?"

"And? And nothing. The car from Mike. It's outside. Tony's in the middle of putting in new seats." I try to sound casually dismissive, but by now the traitorous flush has attacked my neck and face.

"Your son is right," Tony says.

"Well, this should have been completed by now."

Quick, clumping footsteps sound a brief reprieve. In a second the door opens and men move quickly to the time clock. Bonner Senior takes advantage of the noisy flow. "Why didn't you get on this earlier?" he enunciates, facing me in an exaggerated way so that Tony can't read his lips. "We have an auction on Monday, remember?" His eyes attempt to pull a comprehending nod out of me.

My own eyes want to oblige, but they're suddenly riveted to a spot on the desk. Looking at it from my father's point of view, I can imagine how he feels. My blank sockets must resemble a stalled slot machine; no doubt the butt of his hand is twitching with the urge to unjam me.

But he regards me impassively. Control is his only expression. "You didn't forget that, did you?" It's a question, but it's asked in the imperative voice.

I look up at him, completely lost. It's like one of those school amnesia dreams. My skin is a mess. I imagine by now there's a violet tinge to the redness. "Is this ringing a bell?" my father finally asks.

Yeah, it's ringing a bell. A school bell. And I'm getting one of those school sweats. MBA classes don't look so good right now. I pretend to watch the men clocking out, check to see they're doing it right. As they pass my desk, they nod respectfully but wordlessly to my father and sneak a quick eyeful of me.

Bonner Senior's eyes and mouth clamp shut, vents closing

down to prevent steam from escaping. He's aware of the presence of these men, so he begins a soft explanation about the
auction on Monday.

Men are still beating a path by our desk. Bonner Senior
keeps his back to them as he talks to me. But he can feel their
glances lingering longer than necessary, and once in a while
he turns around to face them. This is enough to shoosh them
away. Tony stays in the corner, rocking stiffly on his bowlegs.

"Okay," I say after the explanation. "I'm up to speed now."

Bonner Senior sits down slowly and gives me a sorrowful
look. I can't stand to meet his gaze. I turn to Accounts Payable and flop through the bills. "It's here somewhere," I say,
though I haven't a clue what I'm referring to. I scatter some
invoices around, I check my bottom drawer, which contains
nothing but food. I do anything to avoid looking up into his
face. Bowlegged Tony is standing like a wishbone, taking it
all in. "Okay, so . . ." I mumble. I stand up. "I guess we'd
better get started."

Bonner Senior pushes back his chair in obvious relief.

"There's a problem of odor," Tony says.

"You heard the man, Tony." Bonner Senior's already at the
door.

Outside, I see that our night watchman has arrived. Mr.
Joe Greenslade is talking with Marcus, the only other worker
who hasn't scattered homeward.

"Joe," my dad acknowledges.

Mr. Greenslade bows. He's old, and he has slow, elaborate
manners.

"I've got something I want you to do," Tony tells him.
Greenslade bows deeply. Tony motions for him to follow but
Greenslade heads for the stairs, oblivious. Tony is forced to
pull him off the bottom step to make his point. Greenslade
hangs onto the railing and stands for a few seconds to get his
bearings. He's an old man. Balance is a problem with him.
But he's not annoyed. There's a big smile on his face.

Meanwhile, Bonner Senior is pointing Tony toward the car. "Come here," Tony says to all of us. Marcus, at least, is willing to edge closer. I throw my support to Marcus and leave Bonner Senior standing alone. "I want to show you something," Tony says. "Just come here."

We get closer to the car. An odd smell creeps into the edges.

"That can be taken care of," Bonner Senior informs us when he sees our faces cringing.

Tony hides his nose inside the collar of his shirt. He stands as far from the trunk as possible. With his left foot poised to run, he uses his right arm to flip open the trunk.

"Jesus! God!" The smell is overpowering. We immediately run in the opposite direction, stumbling over Greenslade, who's still shuffling toward the car. At a safe distance we turn around.

"Guess I'll head home now, Mr. Bonner," Marcus says.

Mr. Greenslade is the only one who doesn't want to escape. He steers himself back on course after being run into, and slowly makes his way through the dizzy landmines of middle and inner ear disturbances until he's next to the car.

"See I told you!" Tony shouts with excitement. "His smeller's gone."

"I got vertigo is all," Greenslade says, leaning on the car.

"Look at him! It doesn't bother him. He's perfect for the job."

Once his balance is restored, Greenslade looks into the trunk and smiles. His old body is built like a stepladder, straight but on a slant. At one time he must have been a strong man. His pelvis is wide for a male, though with no flesh on his buttocks, and his back, shrunken from arthritis, is now planted in his hip bed at a size too small. Though he's officially our night watchman, his main job is to dial 911 if something goes wrong enough to wake him. I'm not sure he can even handle that. He talks with a stutter, whether from excitement, old age, or a speech impediment I haven't a clue.

Yes we tried getting younger ones, but they have a problem called not showing up. We were thinking of just bagging it and getting a guard dog instead, a Doberman or a German Shepherd, but the wild dogs put an end to that notion. The theory of the wild dogs is that they used to be respectable pets that somehow "turned." Apparently they're now like a gang of hoodlums on a rampage, corrupting other innocent canines in their path, their numbers ever growing. Nobody wants a guard dog that might become one of their new recruits.

Greenslade removes his head from the trunk of the car. "S-s-s-ome . . . went on here," he remarks. He turns to Bonner Senior with a dry laugh.

"There were a couple of bodies in there for a while," the Senior says. Mr. Greenslade lifts his head. "I say there was a corpse in there."

Greenslade nods knowingly. "Thought so," he says. He starts his shuffle over toward my dad. Marcus's ears perk up at the mention of corpses, and he shuts the door to his pickup and slides over.

Greenslade's got his thumb jerking over his shoulder, and his head bouncing away to the rhythm of his stutter. But he can't get the words out.

"What bodies?" Marcus asks.

Tony's flipping his hands at everyone. "I know this story already." He puts his face down to Mr. Greenslade's. "A *man* body and a *girl* body." He intertwines his fingers and thrusts them up to the old man's eyes.

Greenslade rubs his kidneys while he considers this. "W-w-w-w they engaged to be married?"

"They were either engaged, Joe, or they were married already." Bonner Senior shrugs soberly, the best answer he can give to a good question. I watch him as he tells the story to the group. He's a man in charge with a studied version of the common touch. Physically he looks like the type who always plays the sheriff on TV westerns like *The Big Valley* or *Bo-nanza*—thick whitish hair, stately, retirement handsome, authoritative but deferential to the right people, the Barkeleys, the Cartwrights, and Mike Charny at the county attorney's.

The story, as the sheriff relates it, is that a man and a woman from North Carolina were going to buy some marijuana. They were dealers. "Do you believe it?" Tony interrupts. "Small time." But for having heard it all before, Tony remains pressed to my father's side for the rest of the story. In no time his tough face inherits the look of a child.

"Anyway, the woman was driving," the Senior continues. "The man was in the passenger seat with a briefcase of money. The supplier told him to come back into the garage. When he did, somebody with an Uzi was waiting for him."

"Was he a, a . . ." Greenslade starts to ask but spots Marcus, who is black, and stops.

"A Mexican," my dad says.

"Yeah," Greenslade agrees happily. He grins reassuringly at Marcus.

"He opened fire and killed the guy. The woman of course had no chance to escape. She knew she was done for."

"Yeah," Tony chuckles. They're coming to his favorite part. "What happened?"

"Shot her up right in the car. About sixteen bullets."

Greenslade has to bend over, his delight is so great. He gets dizzy again and Marcus helps him straighten up.

"They caught the men, by the way," my father adds. "And listen to this explanation. The guy claims he didn't mean to shoot them. His finger kept slipping."

"Yeah right . . . ," Tony agrees.

Marcus stretches out his chin to ask something.

"They hid them in the trunk, Marcus," my dad preempts. "A couple of weeks at least."

Marcus, satisfied, retracts his neck.

"Oh," my dad remarks, "here's something interesting. When they did the autopsy on the woman, guess what they found? An old bullet in her from a previous run-in. An old bullet, Joe. She'd been shot before."

With this, Greenslade—barely recovered from his last jag of laughter—is forced to sputter anew.

"He likes hearing about dead girls," Tony says. He stares at Greenslade's shaking body. Then he pokes him.

"Don't poke," my dad says.

Greenslade waves him off, still laughing. "It's all right. W-w-w-where was that bullet located?"

"Turns you on, don't it?" Tony's saying.

"I don't know, Joe," my dad answers. "Near the heart, I imagine. Too dangerous to remove."

"In the chest," Mr. Greenslade observes.

I decide to put an end to this. "Well, this an interesting story, it's all well and good, but the fact remains that you'll never get the stink out."

"It smells?" Greenslade asks.

Tony rolls his thumb toward the old man. "I told you!"

"I don't mind driving it," the old man offers.

"I'll keep that in mind, Joe." My dad accords him a weighty nod.

"We don't need anyone to *drive* it, dingbat!" Tony yells.

Greenslade shakes his head, thoroughly amused. "Dingbat . . ." he mutters.

I leave the group to their merriment and head for the stairs. Once inside the office I call Sharon and tell her I'll be a little late. I'll just meet her and the others at the fern bar she's got picked out. She says okay. Is she withdrawn or simply unannoyed? It's not like her to be calm. "Are you alone?" I ask. She hangs up on me. She's probably alone wishing she weren't. It's my fault. She wants a baby that looks like Bonner Senior. Strong planed features, unethnic but nicely tanned, no freckles. Dark brown hair. But I tell her, Look at my mother and that's what you're going to get. You're going to get a redhead, it's like a tungsten gene, it's strong, it'll burst through anything.

Bonner Senior opens the door and goes through his midwinter stomping routine again. "I've got them fixed up with some industrial-strength cleaner. That should keep them busy." He takes a seat across from me. "It's true. Old Joe Greenslade doesn't smell a thing. It's mighty peculiar." This sounds kind of like *Bonanza* talk. He crosses his legs; then his arms. "Marcus has gone home," he adds. "You'll have to get some lime to deodorize it."

I poke my chin toward the phone. "Had to call Sharon."

He leans quickly over my desk. "Can you do that?" His eyes flicker at me, accusatory, searching; long-suffering. "The lime?" He fastens me with another look, the kind of look aching to be topped off with a cowboy hat. "Don't put Tony in charge of it. Do it yourself. Tony's a welder. End of story." He falls back in his chair.

"You don't have him on a welding job right now," I say, a real edge of anger in my voice. "But you don't seem to mind that." I try to control the heat in my face by flipping through a gift catalog. A Master Desk Appointment Log bespeaks my position in the world with its aura of authority. It promises a quantum leap forward.

I can feel my dad's eyes burning through me as I try to appear engrossed in the World Holiday Labels, an easy way to remember important holidays in different countries. Of course, the red blotches have started and it's clear I'm not engrossed in anything.

"Look," my dad begins. "If you're not happy in your job . . ."

"If you're not happy with the job I'm doing," I retort.

His back and arms push the chair to its maximum give. "I'm happy with the job you're doing." He holds up his hands to stop me from butting in. "For the most part. I just think you need"—the chair squeaks up and down—"a little more management skill."

Have Chris set up NY appointment. Study ad campaign of Sloane. Set up executive vacation schedule. I read from the list of sample entries on the Master Desk Appointment Log. They've even got them handwritten. This is management skill. I close the catalog and toss it aside.

"Enough of that kind of talk," Bonner Senior announces. "We'll get you straightened out. Any news on the home front?" His chin indicates the phone.

"No," I say. "Sharon's fine."

"But no new news to report?"

"No new news."

"Okaaay." He stretches and stands up. "Any plans on the docket tonight?"

"Going out with some friends. Nothing major."

"Well, according to your mother, she has something planned for me. Dinner, I guess. Or a movie. We'll see. Got to keep them happy, right? I'm willing to go along with it."

This is what I hate most, I want to tell him. Because you have good things to tell me about metal shredding doesn't mean you have good things to tell me about life.

He opens the door and waves without turning around. I get up, watch him go down the steps and into his car. He backs the car up to Tony and Mr. Greenslade, hangs out the window with his instructions, then gives them the same kind of blind wave as he drives off.

I stand at the top of the stairs. Greenslade's got the hose out and is spraying into the trunk. "Are you guys almost finished?" I yell. They don't hear me so I clamber down the steps. A piece of paper floats in the air and I clamp it down with my foot. When I stoop to pick it up, I retrieve a hundred-dollar bill. The first thing I do is stuff it in my pocket, stand up straight, check to see if anyone saw me, and run back up the stairs. I lean against the office wall and huff from nerves and exertion. I am seriously out of shape. I take out the hundred-dollar bill and examine it. It's Benjamin Franklin and he's staring right at me. Is this Uncle Sam's way of keeping you honest—aren't the lower denominations kind of profiles? I put the bill back in my pocket, but then I can't help myself. I slip it out again and bring it up to my nose. It smells. It smells bad.

A clod of gravel sprays against the office window. Tony's outside hollering. I open the door. "Come here! Come here!" he's screaming. "Jesus, come here!"

Money is flying in all directions from the trunk. "Get it out, man!" Tony is yelling to Greenslade, who's frantically unearthing the trunk's bowels. Even all that money can't bring Tony closer to the trunk. He runs up to the office and flies back down with a trash bag. "Get it all!" he orders Greenslade, whose inept clawing is annoyingly ineffective. Yet neither of us can help. The smell has drawn a hostile border around the car. "Thank God for no brains," Tony says. He jogs up and down with nerves as he watches Greenslade from a safe distance.

By the time we get all the money collected, it's twilight. We rush up to the office, Greenslade a few minutes behind, and Tony looks in the bag like a kid looking at his Halloween candy. "How're we going to count all this? Man, it stinks. Greenjeans is going to have to do it. In the meantime . . ." Greenslade opens the door, out of breath. "You're going to have to count this, old man, it's too stinky for us. Okay? In the meantime, we'll divide it up." Tony disappears into the toilet. He comes out with two more plastic bags. "Anybody have any objections?" He cocks his head in a question mark.

Greenslade and I keep quiet.

"Fine," Tony shrugs. He hands the two empty garbage bags

to Mr. Greenslade, dumps the third bag upside down. We watch as tens, twenties, and hundreds come streaming out. Tony looks down at it and up at Greenslade. "You're not busy this evening, are you, Greenjeans?" The old man chokes on his laughter. "Here. You're the only one can stand to touch the stuff."

"W-w-w-w-w."

"Count," Tony says.

"Oh yeah," Mr. Greenslade mutters. He bends laboriously and struggles after a hundred-dollar bill.

"Not now. Never mind, go ahead."

A bubble of snot starts to fall from Greenslade's nose. He wipes it off with the bill. "God," I mutter and roll my eyes at Tony.

"Yeah, just mix it up with the dead meat, old man."

"What?" Greenslade asks.

"I said, Think you'll finish by morning at that pace?"

Greenslade bounces his head in amusement. He slaps Tony the jokester on the shoulder. Tony backs off. "Please," he says. "I got to get home and take a shower. Hey, I should pull out a couple of these hundreds for my date tonight. Man, I liked the part about the extra bullet in that girl's tit. Do you think it's true?"

"I imagine," I say.

"It kind of turns me on. Doesn't it turn you on, your old lady with a bullet in her tit? Hey! Greenjeans! Does Mrs. Greenjeans have an old bullet in her tit?"

"I w-w-wish." He chuckles and again goes for Tony's shoulder, but Tony's too quick for him. He heads for the door and I follow. Greenslade's bent body chases us like a slave. "Hey hey, Tony. M-m-my w-wife hasn't got an old bullet, she's just g-g-g an old tit."

"Ha ha that's great, Mr. Greenjeans, tell it to Captain Kangaroo. Don't forget to count the money."

Greenslade stands at the top of the stairs and watches us go down. All of a sudden he rears back and laughs as loud as his old dry throat will allow him.

"Are we leaving?" I ask Tony at the bottom of the stairs.

"Yeah."

"But what are we going to do?"

"Get back here early in the morning. It's Saturday, no-body'll be here."

"Then what?"

"Then. Then nothing. Then it's our money."

"But," I say. But, I want to scream, how do we do it? What if we get caught? How do we get rid of hundred-dollar bills? Where do we go? How much at a time?

So instead I say, "What about the old man? Can we trust him?" I recognize the line from a TV show the night before.

Tony waves me off. "Hey, Greenjeans, no cheating up there. Don't let that money start talking to you."

Greenjeans lifts his head and emits a dry sound. His hands are on his hips. He looks happy.

"And don't tell anyone!"

Very deliberately Greenslade draws a line across his lips. "M-m-my l-lip . . ."

"Yeah we get it. Look, what can I tell you? He doesn't have a brain. Who knows if he can even count."

"That's what I'm worried about," I say.

"When the stink dies down, you count yours and I'll count mine. It can't be that much. It's just dope money for Christ's sake. That's been out for years. Figures somebody from North Carolina would be into marijuana in 1987. Wearing bell-bottoms, right . . . I hated hippies, man, but now I'm one myself. Still running against the wind." Tony begins to sing.

"Has this happened to you before?" I ask. "I mean, it's not really the counting I'm worried about. I mean . . ."

Don't make me do it, Tony, I think. Don't make me whimper.

"Everything will be all right," Tony answers. "Tomorrow

we'll get here real early, we'll go about it very logic-minded. We won't do anything in a hurry. We'll send Greenjeans on his way, and then you and me will pour some after-shave on our money and figure out what to do. You can't count on Greenjeans anyway, he'll walk into a store and stink it up to high heaven, we just got to hope they think he's been stuffing it under his mattress."

"But don't you think we should do it tonight?"

"We can't do anything until we get rid of some of that smell. Are you willing to touch it?"

I shake my head.

"Besides . . . it's late."

A dog howls in the distance.

Tony jerks around. "Did you hear that?"

The dog howls again, followed by a chorus. The sound razors the back of my neck.

Tony rubs himself nervously. "They smell it. Shit, man, this is like a werewolf movie. They're after my meat, man. Hey, Greenjeans! Them dogs is out. Stay inside. We'll close the gate."

Greenslade stays locked in his stance, that of a happy witless housewife admiring her laundry line.

"Get back inside! I said. Them dogs is out. We'll shut the gate."

Finally Greenslade throws back his head in a rasp of comprehension. His chuckle saws the quiet night air. Another dog howls.

Tony's bouncing up and down. "I'm waiting for you, Bonner. I got the smell all over my jeans. Oh Jesus, let's go."

Tony jumps in his car. He pulls out of the gate and parks across the street. I pull in front of him. We both hop out and run across the street to the main gate, swinging it out onto the road before shutting it. "I can feel those dogs," Tony's saying. His hands are shaking as he fiddles with the gate chain. "They're after me," he says.

"Calm down, Tony."

A rustle in the bushes propels us into the air. We twirl and come down frozen, backs pressed into the fence. When nothing happens, my hand unglues itself from the wire mesh and clamps the lock. I keep my eyes ahead. "Do you really think the dogs are coming?"

"Yes, man! They're smelling the meat. They got Thompson, didn't they? They got a taste for humans."

Even Tony pauses at this last remark. Then we take off running for our cars, laughing hysterically. When I get inside and lock the door, the hysteria turns to hyperventilation. Without thinking, I take out my hundred-dollar bill and bring it up to my nose like smelling salts. The fumes clear my head. They really clear my head. My mind is working now, it's watching Tony strut into the bank and give himself away with his hairy welding-speckled arms. A guy like that wouldn't have money, they'll know it, the bank'll know it, the bank's been trained, they know the way money smells when its been festering with a corpse. A chimera suddenly flits through the night; it sends me to the floor. It couldn't get any worse. Now I'm dog meat. The car is rocking. I tell myself: The car may be rocking but the door is locked, calm down. When I resurface, Tony's face is pressed against the windshield. For a moment we stare at each other's distorted features.

"Can't you start your car?" he's yelling.

I roll down the window. "How are we going to cash it?" I ask.

"It's cash. Cash. It's already cashed."

"But you can't . . ."

"After the scent dies down. Don't worry. We'll talk tomorrow." Tony looks around fearfully. "What's wrong with your car? Please, man, don't make me stand here any longer."

"Nothing's wrong. I'll start it up. Let's go."

"I'll follow you home. I'm right behind." He jogs toward his car. "Do you have after-shave?" I call to him. *I got after-shave*

I hear echoed back to me. "Would you pick up some lime too for the car?" I yell. In the dark I see his body pumping.

No stories tonight, I tell myself. Sit quietly at the fern bar and don't turn red. No spinning yarns about the Shredders. Let your friends do the talking. Don't start on the dogs. It'll lead to other things, a taste for humans—don't even start. Stay sober. Talk about adoption.

I turn on the engine and pull out. Now and then I look up to see if Tony's still behind me. His headlights bounce off the rearview mirror and catch me in the eyes. He's got his brights on but I don't mind. It keeps me running smoothly, steady on the road.

FROM

WHERE

I SIT

In the third grade I appeared on *The Uncle Sylvester Show*, a local program filmed live each afternoon. The show consisted of cartoons and a few games. It featured a studio audience of cheering Cub Scouts, Brownies, Camp Fire Girls, and members of assorted other tribes. I was a Bluebird. The Bluebird friend sitting next to me was Jane.

Uncle Sylvester, the star of the show, retained a goofy sidekick named Private Beanhead. Private Beanhead had the dutiful gangliness of most sidekicks, but in all other ways he was disobedient. At least once during every show Uncle Sylvester was forced to pull Private Beanhead's handlebar mustache to curb his sidekick's incorrigible antics, things like squeezing into a bleacher seat between two giggling Brownies.

Uncle Sylvester was a bit more avuncular, as his name implied. He wore gray hair with bangs, a look that inspired no controversy despite the fact that the Beatles were currently sporting the exact same style. He was rounder and heavier, solid-looking but soft. Someone whose lap a child could sit on. But that was from a distance. Up close I found myself recoiling, hoping he would stay away from my side of the bleachers. There was something else that did not translate onto the home viewer's TV screen and that could only be glimpsed firsthand: Uncle Sylvester's mouth had a tendency to gather saliva when he talked. After a few sentences his lips would glisten greedily. Sometimes a mist would escape his mouth as he spouted directions during the commercials and cartoons, referring to us often as "good boys and girls." His hands opened and closed at us with the rapacity of a miser being held back from his coins. Once on screen, however, he kept his hands locked inside his belt at the small of his back. As he faced the camera, those of us behind him watched the fabric of his pants dance in and out like piano keys. This was what interested me most—all the things the camera could not catch.

At the end of every *Uncle Sylvester Show* the kids were rewarded for their enthusiasm with the Round-Up. The Round-Up was when the camera caressed each face individually. Large TVs were positioned at each end of the bleachers so the children could see themselves as they appeared. The jolt of their own faces on a TV screen sent the girls into a one-syllable giggle before straightening quickly into the friendly wave and smile they had been practicing for days. With the boys it was a different story, muggings and antics, the kinds of things that get knowing, long-suffering nods from elementary school teachers.

Meanwhile the mothers stood offstage watching another TV; their dark outlines could be seen fluttering in the recess of the studio. With no such invention as the video cassette recorder to immortalize their babies, the mothers crammed together and grabbed at the moment as if it were champagne gulped from the bottle.

After every face had been panned, the boys and girls began a restless thumping. Everyone knew what happened next. At the conclusion of Round-Up, the camera flew about for several seconds and then alighted upon a single face. The owner of the face received a prize and the show ended.

I sat quietly and waited. Of all the people there, I was probably the only one who didn't want to win. I willed the long neck of the camera lens to turn away. But it kept swinging back, alighting upon me in brief teases. When the camera finally stopped moving, there I was, encircled on the television screen. Uncle Sylvester and Private Beanhead came running around to my seat. In the distance I saw the fluttering of mothers turn inward. They were searching out my mother as though they would know her instantly, the same way you would know the single black mother belonging to the single black child. I'm handicapped, and people expected my mother to match.

After the show Jane's mother offered me a hug. I liked Mrs. Gilbert but I was not ready for another adult's touch, having still on me the gooiness of Uncle Sylvester's wiggling fingers while he asked my name. His grip on the back of my neck grew tighter with each question. I had squirmed to escape but he had immobilized me.

As we filed offstage Private Beanhead and Uncle Sylvester mustered the last light of their star personae to shuffle us out of the studio. A bored limpness soaked Private Beanhead's comic, rubbery body. Beside him Uncle Sylvester appeared to be biting a bullet. The tension provided the first angles to his spongy face. But he used his clamped jaw to good effect: the expression of holding back pain also passed as concern for the children as he nodded silently. His cupped hands moved up and down like someone calmly redirecting a water leak; it was, I assume, to keep the spurting children at bay. One of the departing Cub Scouts jumped to honk Private Beanhead's enormous nose, and Private Beanhead tilted his head heavenward with a grimace of imprecation. His nose, reared back, revealed two cavernous pyramids. Later my mother told me Private Beanhead was also the news weatherman, and I began following the weather just to glimpse those impressive nostrils again.

On the way home we went to McDonald's. Jane and her mother went with us. We parked and walked up to the take-out window. I wore braces on my legs and when I walked I bounced up and down. My sister said I looked like I was riding one of those horse sticks. Often my arms flew up with the effort, but that was controllable if I concentrated. Otherwise I looked fine. I was described as having a very pretty face, although the compliment is such an established insincerity that even a third grader develops an anxiety about just the opposite being true. But sometimes when I was lined up next to their own daughters, mothers bent toward my mom, and with a bit of confidential surprise remarked upon my delicate features. I would feel slightly more reassured.

My mother, who usually balked at paying the extra three cents for a tiny cup of ketchup, sprang for two. We gathered up our sandwiches, French fries, drinks, and extra ketchup, and settled down on a picnic bench. I opened up my hamburger and looked at the pickles. Just looking at them, their diaphanous green texture coagulated with ketchup, was a great pleasure of mine. My embarrassment at having been roped in by the Round-Up was over. I was happy. I turned around to check the arches. The numbers hadn't changed since my last visit—over 9 million hamburgers had been sold.

"It's still the same," Jane said.

"I wonder if we're the next millionth hamburger," I said. "Maybe they'll change the numbers while we're here."

"That would be fun," Jane said.

Next to us, the two adults had begun a soft undercurrent of conversation that I recognized as mother talk. A French fry slid up and down Mrs. Gilbert's lip as she nodded vigorously to my mother's remarks. My mother, for her part, seemed to have carved out several sentences, a whole speech it seemed to me, or at least a paragraph. I had never seen her speak so long without being interrupted. Having friends, I suddenly realized, was different from having a family.

The soothing chords of their conversation glided to a close. Though I couldn't distinguish the words, the glissade at the end indicated a question. Mrs. Gilbert's eyes widened in thought. A ringlet dropping by her temple formed the curve of a question mark. My own eyes grew large in imitation. I felt at my hair and came up against thin straight bangs.

I had always noticed Mrs. Gilbert's coiffure. The styles mothers chose were such a consistent source of disappointment that I had come to view marriage as something to avoid for fear of what it would do to my hair. Mrs. Gilbert's blondish hair was a particular tragedy, I thought. Sectioned out by a home perm, it had taken on a plaid effect. Some swatches hung loosely, fuzzily straight; other swatches had been conscripted into maladroit dollops. Yet her hair so easily could have been beautiful.

My mother's hair, a uniform brown bob, was less startling, with less potential, but neither had she ruined it. It was not the style I would have chosen for me or for my Barbie dolls, but it was a lot better than Mrs. Gilbert's.

I moved up to their faces. It was no contest. There was nothing to say. My mother was beautiful. Mrs. Gilbert was not. She had a pert nose with a slight gully at its tip, and a small chin that trembled when she was excited, as she often was. She was cute, cute enough for jobs in the support services, secretarial, nursing—but not cute enough to strike out on her own. My mother, however, could strike out on her own. That was what I liked to think.

As we got into our cars to go home, I heard Jane telling her mom that we had been hoping to be the next millionth hamburger so we could see them change the sign. It was a long explanation. At the end of it Mrs. Gilbert exclaimed, "That would have been fun!"

They were a team, I saw, a mother-daughter team. I looked over at my own mother. We were a team too. A better team. On the way home my mother told me that the nickname for Sylvester is Sly. "As in sly like a fox," she added.

"Oh," I said. I took this bit of information to heart.

When we pulled into the driveway my dad was under the hood of our second car. His head lifted to view our arrival. Then it dropped down to the engine. Tricked into believing I was safe, I tried to hurry away. But the beam of his flashlight caught me. I didn't know if this was torture or solicitude. I got to watch the gawky hitch of my shadow all the way into the house. Was he playing? Did he want a hug? Was he angry? I was never sure. Angry or in a good mood, it was about the same. Freeze tag, Catch, Hopscotch. He would suggest these games to me in a good mood and when I demurred he would suggest them to me in a bad mood.

The same sort of mercury fluctuated through my sister's veins. She was in the seventh grade and she and her girlfriend Dale DuKane spent all their time in the bedroom, dancing to Beatle records. My mother and I were consigned to eavesdropping through the door. They danced until they stunk up the room with body odor—Dale DuKane body odor, for there was nothing of the smell I could associate with my sister. When it was particularly bad my sister would open the door and call us in to smell it. Dale DuKane would stand in the corner, shyly proud of her accomplishment.

The shyness was deceptive. At least it deceived me; without exactly understanding, I associated shyness with innocence and so, when Dale DuKane became pregnant two years later, I was incredulous. "Shy like a fox," my mother explained. But I refused to believe it. I couldn't fathom it. This so angered my sister that she went after Dale DuKane (they were estranged by this time), found her, and dragged us face to face for a confrontation. With that same expression of shy proudness she had accorded her body odor, she admitted she was pregnant. More importantly, she admitted she wasn't a virgin. I refused to believe either one, so my sister slapped me across the face and pulled me home. In our front yard she ripped off my braces and went inside to throw them at my mother's feet and announce I was several miles away. My mother went screaming through the back door, squealed out the driveway, and spied me standing expressionlessly on the front porch. She didn't say a word, but her face was muscular and taut. My sister ran out singing, "She's been had, she's been had, she's been had!!"

A few nights after my appearance on *The Uncle Sylvester Show*, my sister invited my mother and me into her bedroom. A wild dancing session had left the room incredibly smelly. "Look what Dale Evans DuKane has done!" my sister screeched by way of invitation. She swung out the door like an impresario and a rank blast greeted us.

My mother, not one to waste her opportunities, took advantage of one of the few invitations to enter the inner sanctum. She strode in with clothesline rope and proceeded to tie my sister to the bed in order to cut her bangs. She had me throw my body over her on the bed, counting on my sister's basic good heart to prevent her from kicking me, and thus make the job of hog-tying that much easier. Dale DuKane retreated to a corner and howled. Once my sister was tied up, my mother came at her with the scissors, but my sister twitched her head so violently that poking out her eye became a real possibility and my mother had to desist from her bang-cutting venture. My sister shoved us out the door and threatened to kill us.

In five or ten minutes we crept back to their door and returned to eavesdropping. A fight had erupted over why Dale DuKane hadn't helped my sister when my mother was tying her up. Dale DuKane explained that she was laughing too hard because she thought it was just a joke; when she recovered and saw the danger of the situation, she became afraid for her own bangs. This led to another argument about whose hair was more important and whose bangs were better, meaning straighter (they spent most of their nondancing time taping their bangs with special bang tape).

After leaving them to their bangs argument, my mother chuckled to herself all through the dinner preparations. When Dale DuKane and my sister finally emerged from the bedroom, it was in the heat of battle. They confronted my mother and demanded to know whose bangs were straighter. My mother turned around with a serious face, a neutral face, the kind of face I imagine actors shaking into before the camera rolls—hold it, wait a minute wait a minute, give me a second. Okay. She looked at them and said she thought both sets of bangs were horrible and had made their foreheads all pimply, and then she returned to mashing the potatoes. Both Dale DuKane and my sister screamed with delight. Their shrieks melted right into the whine of the mixer until you couldn't tell machine or human apart. My mother went right on mashing.

When the screams rolled to a finish, I asked my sister why she had cut the bangs off all my Barbie dolls and she and Dale DuKane renewed their shrieks of delight.

But their relationship was not to last long. For people who seemed to enjoy each other so much, they constantly bickered. Their arguments, always hysterical, usually centered around the Beatles. The Beatles were not entirely unrelated to the subject of bangs, however, since Jane Asher—Paul's girlfriend—had an enviable set of straight bangs to go with her straight long hair. Dale DuKane and my sister were filled with venomous jealousy. They wrote letters to Jane Asher calling her a slut, and many more letters to Paul McCartney himself, warning him about the slatternly Jane. They were in agreement about this particular business, but their peace didn't last long. There was the little matter of Beatles lyrics.

In the song "I Want To Hold Your Hand" Dale DuKane claimed the line on the refrain was *I can't hide I can't hide I can't hide!!* My sister, on the other hand, argued that the line was *I get had I get had I get had!!*

My sister, having the strength of her convictions even when wrong, shoved Dale DuKane against the wall. Dale DuKane responded by slapping my sister in the face. A clean crisp shot that left finger marks. Then they proceeded to rip each other's blouses off until they stood in nothing but bras and skirts.

Unfortunately this fight took place in the hallway of our elementary school. Dale DuKane got suspended for three days, while my sister got off with writing a 500-word essay. The topic was "Why Girls Should Not Fight."

Her first sentence was *Girls should not fight in a physical manner because they are younger members of the race known as women.* Every sentence that followed began *Girls also should not fight in a physical manner because in addition to the fact that they are younger members of the race known as women . . .*

In this way the 500-word essay only required about ten sentences. My sister read it aloud to us. Her conclusion was this:

> *Girls also should not fight in a physical manner because in addition to the fact that they are younger members of the race known as women, they could be having their periods and then their cramps might get worse and they would have to go to the nurse and lie down all day and miss important classes such as English, and they would have to call up someone on the phone and get the homework assignment after they got home. Also their period pad could get ripped off, and things might drop out between their legs.*

That was the end of the essay. My mother had shrunk her mouth and appeared to be munching on it as she listened. My sister was especially pleased with her lenient punishment when she found out Dale DuKane had been right all along about the lyrics.

"How do you like it?" she asked my mom.

My mother said, "Mm-hmm."

"What else?" my sister asked.

"Nothing else," my mother said.

"What else?" my sister demanded.

"Get rid of the dropping-out stuff," my mother said.

"Why!" my sister shouted, laughing hysterically. "Stuff drops out between your legs!"

"Hmm," my mother said dryly. She was ready to turn her attention elsewhere. She was not going to give my sister the response she wanted. But I had started giggling and was bent over trying to hide it, and when my mother saw me, a bubble of laughter blew through her lips. Then she stood up to do something official.

My sister followed her. She told her Dale DuKane had hair under her arms and everyone had seen it, that's why she got suspended and not her. My mother didn't react but began filling the sink with clean dishwater. Then my sister turned to me. She demonstrated how Dale DuKane had ripped her blouse to shreds.

"That was an expensive blouse," my mother added, her back to us at the sink.

"The sleeve ripped right off," my sister explained. And for the rest of the day she had been forced to wear her blouse with the sleeve missing.

"They sent you home," my mother corrected.

There was also a ripped front pocket, my sister added, that left a hole just the right size for her boob to go through. She cupped her tiny breast and demonstrated for me. I saw my mother's head turn slightly to take it in. She pruned her mouth to prevent any amusement from showing.

Then my sister told us Dale DuKane had started her period and now she could get pregnant if she kept screwing around with Doug Snow.

My mother said, "Don't use that word."

"What word do you want me to use?" my sister challenged. "You know what I mean."

I was trying to think of Jane and her mother having this conversation. Then I tried to think of Jane's mother and my sister having this conversation. I couldn't imagine it.

My father walked through the room and we fell silent. Although I had been quiet all along, he chose me to look at. He said, "What are you up to?" and I said, "Nothing." He said, "I can't walk in here without someone trying to stir things up," and continued out the door.

My mother started to chase after him, but my sister stopped her and screamed, "You know what word I mean!! Don't pretend you're so innocent!!"

My sister kept bothering her and my mother kept trying to clear her off her shoulder and do the dishes until finally she gave up and stepped outside and called my father's name. Panic creased my sister's face and she ran down the hallway and slammed the door to her bedroom. My mother asked my father to go put gas in the car. My father yelled that he wasn't going to put gas in the car until she stopped stirring things up, and if she didn't stop stirring things up she could run out of gas and then maybe she'd learn.

My mother replied she hadn't been stirring things up, what did he mean by that, and what exactly would she learn if she ran out of gas, how cruel, and he said it wasn't cruelty it was a lesson, and she said, "Oh a cruel lesson!" So began another argument that never had a clear beginning or end.

After my sister turned in her essay with its musings on menstruation, she was reprimanded and punished again. This time she was not given another essay that might allow her creative juices to flood. She was made to write this sentence five hundred times: *If I continue this pattern of disobedience, I will subsequently become a juvenile delinquent.*

My sister diagrammed the assignment in columns and colors. She drew the first column and penciled *If* on every line. Then she drew a second column, took a red pencil, and wrote *I*. She used blue ink for *continue*. By the time she reached the seventh column and the word *disobedience*, it was clear she would not be able to get the whole sentence on one line, something she should have thought of had she bothered to think ahead.

Undaunted, she scotch-taped extra sheaves of paper and widened her margins. By the time she was done, she had something that looked like a road map, words that were interstate-divided, multicolored, and accordion-creased from its mystifying system of folding.

Now that her friendship with Dale DuKane was over, she found a new friend with a rapidity that over the years would never cease to amaze me, especially when it involved men. One of the initiations her new friend had to undergo was learning the sentence *If I continue this pattern of disobedience, I will subsequently become a juvenile delinquent* and repeating it often for my mother's benefit.

The friend's name was Elizabeth Browning and one day her name was Liz, the next week Eliza, then Betsy, Beth, and so on. Each day, as we drove her home, my mother seemed to take pleasure in addressing her at every opportunity by her current name of choice. Elizabeth had tiny sharp features and her face as a whole drew back from its center point, the nose. It was an effect my mother called fox-faced, continuing her fixation with fox analogies. She was anxious to meet Elizabeth's mother, to see if they looked alike.

When they did meet, on a Saturday when my mother was taking the girls to the skating rink, I saw my mother kind of staring at Mrs. Browning and smiling in that hidden way of hers, as if she could already see the beginning, middle, and end of this person's whole rather amusing life. She asked the mother if she had named her daughter after Elizabeth Barrett Browning. Mrs. Browning said she didn't know; her husband had chosen the name.

With this the husband magically appeared at the doorway. He had on a white T-shirt and was holding a beer and did a good job of filling up the whole doorway. My mother turned and asked him if he had named his daughter after Elizabeth Barrett Browning. The husband gave her a blank, beery, not too kindly stare, which slowly rotated and settled on me, and my mother said, "You know, the famous poem, 'How do I love thee let me count the ways.'" After intoning this first line my mother closed her recitation of the poem, not out of fear of Mr. Browning but because she didn't know the rest.

My mother's obliviousness to this frightening hulk in the doorway caused a look of admiration to cross over Mrs. Browning's face, so noticeable that Mr. Browning thundered a warning. "I'm just impressed with her knowledge of books," Mrs. Browning explained, her hands sweeping us like dust balls toward our car. When we left them, I knew my mother had managed to start a big fight in her wake.

On the way to the skating rink my sister asked her to recite the rest of the poem.

"How do I love thee let me count the ways," my mother said.

"That's all you know!" my sister squawked gleefully.

My mother feigned boredom at my sister's screaming. In the backseat my sister jabbed Elizabeth into joining in. From the front seat I watched the impassive face of my mother, the only glimmer of movement the eye muscles moving back and forth to the rearview mirror.

"What do you expect from someone who has stuff dropping from her legs?"

"Stop it."

"Do you deny it?"

"Oh stop it," my mother said wearily, "or I'm dropping you home with Daddy."

"Oh stop it stop it," my sister mimicked. "And if you continue this pattern of disobedience, you will subsequently become a juvenile delinquent and I will subsequently drop you home with Daddy."

"Very funny," my mother said, though I sat beside her giggling.

"Somebody thinks so."

Then my sister prodded Elizabeth into saying, "Don't you think it was mean of Mrs. Latimer to make her write that?"

"No, Betsy," my mother said. "Because that's what she is. She's going to be a juvenile delinquent."

"My name isn't Betsy," Elizabeth said. "It's Beth."

"And I would thank you for addressing me by that name," my sister prompted.

"And I would thank you for addressing me by that name," Elizabeth repeated.

"How do I name thee, let me count the ways," my mother said.

"Very funny in case you were wondering."

"You asked me to recite the poem," my mother said.

"Could you speed it up?" my sister demanded.

During these first few rides, as I was getting to know Elizabeth, my sister often browbeat her into exclaiming enthusiasm over my appearance on *The Uncle Sylvester Show*. She herself hadn't bothered to watch the show, due to lack of interest, yet she was inordinately proud of my appearance on it. Years later when I graduated from law school, she swelled with pride but neither attended the ceremony nor watched a single minute of the videotape. My college graduation she showed up for but left during the A's. Just as "Appelbaum" was being called, she bolted up from her chair with a shock of realization on her face. "Oh my God!" I could almost hear her saying. "They're calling every fucking name in alphabetical order!" Appelbaum, who was kind of a nut, grabbed the diploma and ran off like a maniac, escaping almost as fast as my sister. My mother remained blissfully ignorant, having learned by then never to sit near her daughter.

Pinned in the backseat, Elizabeth did her best to praise *The Uncle Sylvester Show*. My sister asked her if she thought I had won the Round-Up prize because I'm crippled, and Elizabeth said no. Then she asked my mother and my mother said no. Then she asked me and I said yes. My sister shrieked wildly at this. Then she asked Elizabeth if she thought I was funny and Elizabeth said she didn't know. My sister repeated this question until Elizabeth said yes. Then my sister asked, "Are you sure?" and Elizabeth said yes to this too. Then my sister told me that Dale DuKane hadn't liked me because I was crippled and this was the real reason she had ripped her blouse off. After a few seconds my sister said, "Just kidding. It was really over the Beatles. Dale DuKane really likes you." And she asked me if I believed her and I said yes. Then she said, "Are you sure?" and my mother said, "Yes, she's sure. We're all sure. Now shut up." My sister started shrieking again and asked my mom why she had done that, didn't she like her? and my mother said, "Oh yes yes yes, now PLEASE."

As usual my sister had worked herself out of control and as the ride ended she was shouting her 500-word essay, which she had memorized and was currently teaching to Elizabeth. *Also their period pad could get ripped off, and things might drop out between their legs!*

My mother swung into the parking lot of the skating rink. "Out," she said.

My sister jammed her up against the steering wheel and shoved her way out. She slammed the car door, almost taking off my mother's hand. Despite this, she turned to wave good-bye. My mother emphasized a wide *H* as she pulled the steering column gearshift into first and aimed the wheels at the two girls. My sister's mouth formed a round donut of terror and delight, and she and Elizabeth Browning took off through the parking lot with our car steadily behind.

"I'm worn out," my mother said. "How does she get like this?"

I was privy to these conversational asides since she had no one else to listen to her. "Did you notice Elizabeth's mother is fox-faced like her?" she asked me as we continued chasing them through the parking lot. I watched my sister laughing so hard she constantly stumbled in her running. I never felt so happy. I loved getting to ride along in the front seat and listen to things I shouldn't be hearing. Whenever my mother was driving them anywhere I would grab my braces like others grab their coats and flounder toward the car in a panic, braces half on half off, afraid they wouldn't wait. "Go horsey go!" my sister would yell out the window, constantly trying to get my mother to pull out of the driveway as though she were really leaving without me. During these times I felt no need to have a friend of my own along; in fact, without one, there was more of a reason for me to cling to the shadow of my sister and Elizabeth.

On a Saturday when the weather was warming up, my mother planned a trip to the Morgan Horse Farm. The drive was more than two hours long; all week I found myself anxiously looking forward to the trip, to the more than four hours I would spend in the car with Elizabeth and my sister, and I purposely neglected to invite any friend of my own.

We started early in the morning with picnic food my mother had prepared the night before. By the time we got to the edge of the city, my sister and Elizabeth had already decimated the sandwiches; however, my mother, anticipating this, had the real bag hidden away.

Once at the horse farm, my mother issued warnings to be-

have to both my sister and Elizabeth. But it was too late. Now
that we were already here, they were going to do anything
they wanted. Which they did. Even before the tour began it
became apparent that the studhorse would garner all their
attention; my mother, also anticipating this, had passed on
our first tour guide, an older woman, and opted for a tough-
looking cowboy. I heard her speak to him in a low voice while
we waited for the right number of people to assemble. One of
his cheeks popped in and out as he nodded to my mother. To
my mother his voice was quiet and respectful, but with my
sister and Elizabeth he was a tyrant with a twang. "I don't
want to hear it from you two," he warned. His hand pointed
to them in the shape of a pistol. They looked to my mother
for salvation from this abuse, but she ignored them.

The end of the tour brought us into the museum. I wandered from there into the gift shop, where my heart sank in
disbelief. Jane and her mother stood over a counter of sou-
venirs. My instinctive reaction was escape. I didn't want to
share my sister and her friend. Of all the places in a two-hour
radius, why were they here?

I turned to leave but the braces and the hitch in my stride
created just enough metal clicking to turn their heads. "Hello
the Boat!" Mrs. Gilbert called excitedly. This was supposed to
be kind of a joke, because I had just loaned Jane a book called
Hello the Boat and it was about early settlers floating down
the Ohio River on flatboats while Indians lined up along the
shore and shot arrows at them. At the sound of her voice I
felt like one of their arrows had pierced me in the back. "Why
hello, hello there!" I turned around with a painful smile.

A large crisp butterfly was pinned to the lapel of Mrs.
Gilbert's jacket. She and Jane wore matching jumpers with
ruffles. Immediately my pain vanished in the urge to hide
them before my sister and Elizabeth caught sight of their sug-
ary clothing.

I felt torn between two worlds, embarrassed to have my

friendship with Jane revealed to my sister and Elizabeth;
afraid for Jane, on the other hand, and the comments my sister might deliver to her directly instead of saving them for the
ride home.

Then my mother walked in and greeted them without hesi-
tation. Now it was Mrs. Gilbert who seemed overtaken by
embarrassment. An untamed curl swung recklessly on her
temple as she issued breathless excuses about having relatives
in the area, otherwise she would have certainly extended an
invitation. Her forehead began to shine. It never crossed my
mind that they should have invited us to come along on their
outing, but seeing an adult break into a mist of perspiration
over her social lapse made me feel all the more guilty, not
just for neglecting to ask Jane but for not wanting to ask
her, for being so overwrought with my sister's and Elizabeth's
presence I would have gladly lied to keep her away.

And so I agreed when Mrs. Gilbert mentioned what a delight it would be for Jane and me if I rode home with them in
their car. Jane smiled shyly. And though I admired Jane, there
was something missing. Looking at Mrs. Gilbert's butterfly, I
felt the deadliness of trying to arrange oneself in a pleasing
manner, but I managed nonetheless to prop myself in their
backseat, pretty as a picture, and wave a pleasant farewell to
my mother. I was miserable. I was with a friend and a very
nice mother, and yet I had never been so unhappy.

Mrs. Gilbert stood in the parking lot enjoying a final few
words with my mother. When she saw Jane and me waiting
for her, her fingers toodled good-bye and she broke into a sort
of a run, a mother's trot, elbows digging into her ribs and
hands flapping aimlessly. My mother immediately turned to
hush my sister and Elizabeth before they had even a chance
to comment.

A girlish excitement shone on Mrs. Gilbert's face. She stuck
her head briefly into the backseat to make sure we felt it

too. Her chin trembled slightly. I wondered if Jane could have
kissed her now had she asked. Would the hint of perspiration
on her forehead repel Jane too? For a moment I looked over
at Jane and wondered how she could stand it, how she could
stand living with her own mother.

For the first part of the trip my mother's car was just in
front of us as we wound along country roads. It seemed so
bulky and slow, like a huge gorged scarab. I tried to picture
my sister and Elizabeth screaming at my mother to speed it
up. Were they talking about us? I wondered. I wished I were
there to listen.

Surprisingly, Mrs. Gilbert drove with only one hand, except on curves. Her free hand roamed her body, from hairline
to eyes to upper lip. Her fingers nibbled at the buttons of
her blouse, ironing the front placket, toying especially at the
area between her breast. All this nervous movement I held
against her.

From the vantage point of the backseat I had a new angle
and unlimited freedom to stare. Once again I studied the particular tragedy of her hair. It could have been so lovely. It was
a brownish golden color with actual yellow streaks, thick and
shiny. Many times I imagined myself having that hair and the
ways I would style it once it was mine. I'd let it hang long
and straight and luxurious. I would not, as Mrs. Gilbert had
done, reel it in like so much tangled fishing wire. I was sick
just thinking about it.

"Oh look," Mrs. Gilbert said.

Up ahead my sister and Elizabeth had turned around and
were pressing their faces to the back window. Mrs. Gilbert
chuckled. "Hello!" she called as though they could hear her.
Then my sister started pumping the finger of one hand through
the ring the other hand formed. Mrs. Gilbert put her hand
close to the windshield and waved back.

The road twisted around the contour of the Appalachian

Mountains. We began climbing, and my mother's car crawled more slowly. I saw my sister and Elizabeth bouncing crazily, obviously yelling at my mother to speed up. Around one of the corners appeared a sign: SCENIC VIEW AHEAD. My mother's car turned into the half circle and stopped. We pulled in behind. When she opened the car door, it was as if a volcano had been unsealed from a vacuum. Instantly there was the shrill explosion of voices. Both Jane and Mrs. Gilbert jumped.

The mothers met at the edge of the half circle and looked out over the valley. They made appreciative remarks to each other about its beauty. My sister and Elizabeth refused to get out of the car. Instead they stayed inside, screeching things like "Scenic View Ahead! Oh my God! Scenic View! The most scenic view of horse wicks in the world!!" Jane had stopped midway between the car and the edge of the escarpment. Each time she edged farther toward the view, the raucous laughter spun her head back to the car and the two people who inspired a strange kind of fear and a strange kind of attraction.

I was more decisive than Jane. I ignored the view completely and walked over to them. "Faster faster!" my sister screamed and I turned around to Jane with a knowing laugh. They may be frightening but I can handle them. *I know these people* was the message I was trying to send. Feeling proud and adult, aware of Jane watching me, I plopped my forearms on the open window and peered in to chatter.

"Having fun with Jane the slut?" my sister asked me. I didn't know what a slut was, but I knew it was the word she used to describe Paul McCartney's girlfriend, Jane Asher.

"Yes," I said.

"So you admit she's a slut?" my sister said.

I looked around. "What's a slut?" I asked. "Just tell me."

"A slut is someone who's crippled," Elizabeth said.

"Watch it," my sister said and slapped her, or tried to.

They locked horns and were suddenly grappled and inter-
twined. Their bodies ground into the floor space and they
disappeared. Was this the end of another friendship?

I called to my mother, who was enjoying her respite of
mother talk with Mrs. Gilbert. I pointed to the car. "They're
fighting," I said. With an almost motionless nod, she managed
to convey her weary dismay. Then she went back to talking
with Mrs. Gilbert. I joined Jane in our no-man's land, midway
toward either group.

The fight must have resolved itself, for in a few minutes
they began to recite my sister's 500-word essay. *Girls should
not fight in a physical manner because they are younger members of the race known as women.*

"All right," my mother quickly said. "We'd better go."

"They're getting restless," Mrs. Gilbert encouraged, though
it was her own face that was dropping little by little as their
recitation chipped away at her genial expression. My mother
stood briefly by the driver's side, and I gave her what I hoped
was a longing look. *Take me with you.* I wanted my face to
shout its message.

I saw a response in my mother's face.

But Mrs. Gilbert's voice innocently chirped in. "We're having a grand old time," she said.

The chanting of my sister and Elizabeth grew louder. They
were fast coming to the final, obscene part of the essay. My
mother flung me an italicized look, a quick look that said *I'm
sorry I've got to go now and you know why.* I searched for a
twinge to her eyes that would mirror my own sadness at being
left behind. But it could hardly matter so much to her that I
was stuck with Jane and Mrs. Gilbert since I would be home
in two hours' time. Perhaps she even believed I was having
fun, just as Mrs. Gilbert did. Would I always be thought of as
having a grand old time when I was really so miserable?

I watched them drive away, trouble and wild moods and

frantic adolescent love on the horizon for my sister, and what for me? Could I sense already that my future contained a procession of humble pleasures which would give more joy to others than to me? That I would be expected to feel my reward from their small kindnesses, to blush tearfully at their prizes or compliments? That warm regard and gratitude were my province, and that the more alarming passions would not be mine?

Paul Rawlins, *No Lie Like Love*
Harvey Grossinger, *The Quarry*
Ha Jin, *Under the Red Flag*
Andy Plattner, *Winter Money*
Frank Soos, *Unified Field Theory*
Mary Clyde, *Survival Rates*
Hester Kaplan, *The Edge of Marriage*
Darrell Spencer, *CAUTION Men in Trees*
Robert Anderson, *Ice Age*
Bill Roorbach, *Big Bend*
Dana Johnson, *Break Any Woman Down*
Gina Ochsner, *The Necessary Grace to Fall*
Kellie Wells, *Compression Scars*
Eric Shade, *Eyesores*
Catherine Brady, *Curled in the Bed of Love*
Ed Allen, *Ate It Anyway*
Gary Fincke, *Sorry I Worried You*
Barbara Sutton, *The Send-Away Girl*
David Crouse, *Copy Cats*
Randy F. Nelson, *The Imaginary Lives of Mechanical Men*
Greg Downs, *Spit Baths*
Peter LaSalle, *Tell Borges If You See Him: Tales of Contemporary
    Somnambulism*
Anne Panning, *Super America*
Margot Singer, *The Pale of Settlement*
Andrew Porter, *The Theory of Light and Matter*
Peter Selgin, *Drowning Lessons*
Geoffrey Becker, *Black Elvis*
Lori Ostlund, *The Bigness of the World*

LaVergne, TN USA
15 October 2009
160913LV00001BA/31/P